Craved by an Alpha

Felicity Heaton

ETERNAL MATES SERIES

Kissed by a Dark Prince
Claimed by a Demon King
Tempted by a Rogue Prince
Hunted by a Jaguar
Craved by an Alpha
Bitten by a Hellcat (Coming February 17th 2015)
Taken by a Dragon (Coming March 10th 2015)

Find out more at: www.felicityheaton.co.uk

CHAPTER 1

Cavanaugh checked his watch. The coloured lights above the bar of Underworld flashed across the glass face in time with the thumping music, but didn't stop him from seeing what he wanted. It was gone midnight. Four years and three hundred and fifty seven days had passed. In eight days, with the rising of the full moon, he would be a man without status.

He couldn't wait.

It felt as if this moment had been too long coming, as if he had been waiting an eternity for it to pass. Pride politics and all the bullshit that came with the territory would cease to exist.

He would be free.

Cavanaugh leaned his backside against the corner of the black bar, tucking himself away from the lighted area off to his left where Sherry was flirting with another group of young fae as she served them their drinks, twirling her blonde ponytail around her fingers, and Kyter was stomping around looking as if he was chewing a wasp. Hard. The big sandy-haired jaguar shifter had been in a foul mood since his new mate, Iolanthe, had returned to her homeland of the elf kingdom to break the news to her parents. Apparently, Kyter had wanted to go with her, and Iolanthe had wisely decided to go alone. Cavanaugh had overheard her mentioning something about how he had threatened to kill her parents.

He sighed and rolled his shoulders to ease the ache building in them, born of a punishing workout session that had lasted over half a day. The closer he came to the day he had been waiting for, the tenser he became and the only release he had found was unleashing hell on the gym Kyter had set up in the back of the nightclub Cavanaugh called home.

His boss had suggested finding a female to slake his needs, but Cavanaugh wasn't interested in the women who frequented the club, or their attention. He could probably have his pick, but there was only one woman he wanted in this world.

His fated mate.

He palmed the right pocket of his black trousers, feeling the wallet there, his thoughts with the faded photograph it contained. The image was seared on his memory, burned there by countless hours spent lying on his bed in his small apartment in the back of Underworld, holding the old picture above him and staring at it.

Countless hours filled with regret.

Countless hours in which he had wondered how different things might have been.

He was trying to make that difference happen. He was trying to change the paths they had somehow ended up treading and bring them back together.

The methods he had chosen hadn't been the best, but he couldn't change things now. He had made his choice and he had lived with it, through the fight that had almost claimed his life to the pain of realising the mistake he had made to the close to five years of separation that had broken part of him.

That part of him had been fractured before he had set in motion the series of events that had brought him to Underworld.

It had been a constant source of pain since that fateful night back at his pride's village and he had been doing his best to stem the flow of it, feeling as if he was trying to hold back a tsunami with his bare hands. Every night since then, he had patched up his heart as best he could and fought for the strength to keep walking forwards, his eyes fixed on the future he wanted, determined to make it happen.

Determined to turn all the mistakes he had made, and the pain and the loneliness he had endured, into something glorious.

Having his mate in his arms.

A commotion near the entrance of the nightclub off to his left caught his attention and Kyter's too. Cavanaugh stared beyond the sandy-haired male, trying to catch a glimpse of what was happening. The crowd was too thick, the club jumping tonight, making it impossible to catch anything other than a flash of a tattered grey coat hood and a backpack. It looked as if someone had rolled into the wrong place.

They were dressed for a damned expedition, not a nightclub where most of the patrons wore little and worked up a sweat on the dance floor, and in the shadowy alcoves.

A female flagged him, waving her hand as if he was a slave and she could order him around. Cavanaugh shot her a black look but she persisted, flashing him a come-get-me smile that made him cold inside.

No one could smile as *she* could.

Her smile lit up the world.

It made even the coldest reaches of his heart warm.

The smile she wore in the picture in his wallet, her arms wrapped around his neck and her rosy cheek pressed against his. She had hurled herself into his arms when her mother had offered to take a photograph of them to test out the camera he had bought for her as a present from his latest trip down the mountain to the nearest big town. He had been gone for a week and gods he had missed Eloise in that time.

2

Gods he had missed her since fleeing the village five years ago, his pride in tatters but resolve burning in his heart.

Hope that he might be able to carve out the future he wanted, escaping the one he had been born into and forced to accept.

He was about to give up and serve the female still frantically trying to get his attention when the hooded trekker moved closer. His gaze zeroed in on them over the heads of the patrons lining the busy bar.

It was a woman. Average height. A little too thin even with the thick coat. She stumbled into a group of five male demons near the edge of the dance floor off to his left and waved her small hands around, flashing scars that circled her wrists.

When one of the burly demon males lightly pushed her shoulder, barely touching her, she staggered back and almost fell but recovered herself. What was wrong with her?

Was she a homeless person, on drugs, or maybe drunk?

She was unsteady on her feet as she backed away from the demons, heading in Cavanaugh's direction, towards one group of the thick black columns that rose up on either side of the dance floor to support the high ceiling of the club. The demons followed her, exchanging glances and wicked smiles that made Cavanaugh wonder what the female looked like. Her hood obscured her face, hiding it from him, but he guessed she was pretty because the demons looked as if they wanted to party with her.

She waved her hands again as she moved directly in front of Cavanaugh, clearly trying to deter the males, and he sensed the fatigue rolling off her. Not drunk or on drugs. She had stumbled because she was weak.

His dark grey eyes began to widen.

He could sense her fatigue?

Her scent hit him hard, knocking him back a step, and he had to grab the edge of the black bar top in front of him to steady himself. He stared at her, unable to take his eyes off her, his head and heart reeling.

It couldn't be.

The demons tossed her black scowls when she flashed them something. A small square of paper.

The tallest of the group pointed towards the bar.

She turned.

Cavanaugh's heart stopped.

Wavy dark hair spilled from beneath the hood, the lights from the club playing over the lower half of her face, turning her pale skin different colours as she searched the length of the bar.

Eloise.

He dug his emerging claws into the wooden bar top to anchor himself, holding himself back as a fierce need to go to her swept through him and battling the waves of disbelief that crashed over him.

His heart said that she was nothing more than a fantasy. She was a figment of his overwrought imagination brought about by thinking of her too much, planning how he was going to make things up to her once he was free of his status and returned to the village, and how he was going to break it to her that she was his fated female. She couldn't be here. It wasn't possible.

His head and every instinct he possessed said that she was. She was real.

And she was as beautiful as he remembered, with her soft heart-shaped lips that made him yearn to kiss her, her impish button nose and her striking eyes framed by long dark lashes.

Looking at her now, he couldn't believe he had managed to live so long without seeing her or smelling her scent, but the sight of her made the short time they had been apart feel more like an eternity than ever.

He breathed hard, clutching the bar top as he waited for her, his heart labouring as he silently willed her to notice him, even as he feared it at the same time. He knew she would be angry with him for leaving the pride and leaving her, and that making her understand his reasons was going to be difficult. He didn't expect her to forgive him straight away, but he was willing to work to win her back.

She was all that mattered to him.

He didn't give a damn about his position or the pride. There was only one reason he regretted leaving the village. There was only one reason it had killed him to leave.

It had killed him to leave her.

But she was here now. She was standing only metres from him, back within his grasp but still beyond it at the same time.

He cursed the gods.

They had given him both his wildest dream and his worst nightmare. Eight days. Why couldn't they have brought Eloise to him in eight days, when he was free to be with her?

Waiting those eight days was going to be torture, but he would endure it. He would fight every instinct that demanded he claimed his mate, because she deserved to be cherished and treasured. She deserved to know that he loved her and what they had was real.

She deserved to have a choice and not feel obliged to be with him because he was her alpha and pride rules dictated she should give herself to him if he expressed an interest in her.

It wasn't the relationship he wanted for them. He needed to know that she was with him out of choice, not because of his position.

He needed her to know that he respected her, loved her, and that she was the only female for him.

He wanted no other.

In eight days, that would be possible. He would be free to be her mate.

Right now, the laws of their kind dictated she could only be his mistress.

He would never do such a thing to his Eloise. He would never dishonour her in such a way or treat her as if she was his inferior. As much as it killed him, he would wait for her.

He would wait forever if that was what it took.

Another of the demons, a handsome dark-haired male, clapped a hand down on her shoulder and pulled her back around to face him, a seductive smile curving his lips.

The acrid tang of fear tainted her sweet scent.

Cavanaugh snarled and reacted on instinct. He pressed one hand into the bar top and easily vaulted it. The patrons on the other side gasped and rushed out of his path, and he landed silently on his booted feet. He shoved through the crowd, not caring how many fae or demons he pissed off as he made a beeline for her and the male who had dared to frighten her.

He pushed the last of the patrons out of his way and had his hand on her arm a heartbeat later. A thunderbolt zinged along his bones, setting him on fire and detonating the ticking bomb that was his temper. He growled through his emerging fangs as he yanked her behind him, tearing a gasp from her, and placed himself between her and the demons.

He slammed the flat of his other palm against the demon's broad chest, shoving him into the four behind him. The demon growled at him, a corona of fire around his irises warning Cavanaugh that he was close to changing, his horns on the verge of emerging and revealing what he was to the humans around them.

Cavanaugh snarled back at him, the club brightening as his eyes began to transform, turning silver. His blood pounded and every instinct he possessed roared at him to protect Eloise. He fought the fierce need to shift, battling his snow leopard form as it writhed beneath his skin, stirred by his hunger to rip the demon male to shreds with his claws.

The demon straightened to his full height, standing almost five inches taller than Cavanaugh's six-foot-six, and stared him down. Cavanaugh didn't flinch. He held the male's gaze as it brightened too, beginning to glow red. One of the male's friends muttered something and touched his shoulder, and the male looked away from Cavanaugh, glancing beyond him to the bar.

5

Cavanaugh could feel Kyter there, watching what was happening. His silent backup.

He appreciated the support from his boss, especially when the demons cast him one last glare before disappearing into the crowd. He remained still, watching them go, breathing hard to steady himself and calm his need to shift. He would be out of his job, and his home, if his boss had to explain to the local authorities how a snow leopard had suddenly appeared in Underworld.

When the demon males had moved to the edges of his senses, Cavanaugh became aware of his hand and the delicate arm it gripped. He became aware of her where she stood behind him, trembling, and not only because of fear. There was fatigue there too, and something else.

The same reason he was shaking inside?

He had imagined this moment a thousand times or more. It hadn't gone exactly as he had planned and it had come too early, but life loved to screw with him and he would find a way to roll with it.

He drew down a deep breath, held it, and slowly turned to face her.

She lifted her eyes up to his, their striking golden-brown depths hitting him hard. He always had loved them, had been able to stare into them for hours while she talked to him, laughed, and smiled. They expressed all of her feelings.

Tonight they made him feel cold inside.

They were haunted.

Her pain was clear in them.

She dropped her eyes to her feet and he frowned at how she held herself, her free arm tucked against her chest. Defensive. Afraid.

The scars on her wrists caught his eye again and he went to touch them but she edged back a step, placing her free arm beyond his reach. He lowered his hand, not wanting to frighten her or make her feel uncomfortable. He wanted to do the opposite. He wanted to comfort her.

The club crowd closed in again, jostling him. The music pounded, hurting his ears and irritating him. He fought the deep need to flash his fangs at the people around them to drive them away from Eloise to remove some of her fear. He wanted to vanquish it all. His deepest primal instincts demanded he take her somewhere safe in order to make that happen. Somewhere she would no longer feel afraid. Somewhere quieter where they could talk.

Somewhere they could be alone.

He tugged her with him through the crowd, shoving everyone out of his way again as he headed for the bar.

"Someone cover my space?" he shouted over the din as he reached the end of the bar.

Kyter nodded, losing his gloomy air for a second, a look in his golden eyes as he dropped them to Eloise and then pinned them back on Cavanaugh. He would answer the jaguar shifter's questions later. Right now, he needed to know what had happened to Eloise to bring her all the way out here, so far from home.

Had she come for him? Or had she come for a different reason?

His heart said to let it be him, but he didn't dare hope that he was the reason she was here.

He pulled her to his left, into a shadowy corner of the club, and up to the door in the black wall that led into the back. He punched in the code on the silver panel, twisted the knob, and pushed the heavy door open. It was only then he released Eloise.

He held the door for her. She slowly passed him, her pack shifting with each wary step she took into the warmly lit large space that acted as a huge hallway, with doors punctuating the wall to his right that led to the gym, playroom and offices, and a metal staircase against the wall on his left that led up to the apartments for the staff. When she was clear of the door, he stepped through and let it swing shut behind him. It slammed, the sound echoing around the expansive pale room.

Eloise jumped and whirled to face him. The grey hood of her coat fell back with the motion, revealing her to him.

"Sorry," he muttered and she dropped her eyes to her feet again.

Cavanaugh silently cursed her. When he had imagined their reunion, she hadn't been so damned meek. She had been the woman he had known a decade ago, before shit had gone south. She had been as beautiful and radiant as she had been back then too, her eyes bright and not haunted, her skin pale and clear, not scarred around her wrists and dark beneath her eyes.

The sight of her and her behaviour clawed at him, filling him with a dark need to discover what had happened to her and take action against anyone who might have harmed her.

He shook with that need, a storm brewing in his heart, a dangerous tempest that needed a target—someone he could make suffer as Eloise clearly had.

A target other than himself.

Right now, he could only place the blame on his own shoulders and it tore him apart, ripping his heart to shreds and filling his mind with poisonous words, ones that stung and made him bleed.

Eloise would never forgive him.

Eloise would never be his.

CHAPTER 2

Cavanaugh mastered his fear and drove it back into submission, clearing his head of the dark words that taunted him and steadying his heart, reassuring himself that all wasn't lost. Eloise was here with him. She had come for him. He needed to focus on taking care of her and discovering what had happened to her to bring her to London, a world away from their village in the mountains of Bhutan.

"What are you doing away from the pride?" He ventured a step towards her and was thankful when she didn't move away to maintain the distance between them. He needed to be close to her. He needed reality to sink in so he could believe she was here with him, standing in the bright back room of Underworld, and he was talking to her for the first time since he had assumed the role of alpha a decade ago, about to hear her sweet voice again. "What happened to you?"

He reached out and gently caught her wrist, bringing it up between them and luring her towards him. He lightly rubbed his thumb over the scarring on it, marks that looked as if they had been made by ropes. Who had done this to her? Whoever it had been, Cavanaugh was going to find them and tear them to pieces. He was going to make them suffer as she had. A growl rumbled through his chest and curled up his throat, born of a dark and consuming hunger to avenge her.

She pulled free of his grip and hid her arms behind her back.

"Goddammit, Eloise," he barked and she lowered her head, turning her face away from him.

The rich brown waves of her long hair fell down to conceal her face but didn't hide how her shoulders trembled beneath her dirty coat. He reined in his frustration. He could sense her struggle, could smell it in the subtle changes in her scent. It was taking a lot for her to remain silent when she felt compelled to obey the rules of their kind and answer him.

Why wouldn't she answer him? He needed to know what had happened to her. It filled him completely, an incessant urge that he couldn't shake, born of his deep connection to her. He feared he would go mad or lose his temper if she insisted on remaining silent and refused to tell him what had happened to her.

He would go mad if she refused to look at him or give him the pleasure of hearing her voice too. Couldn't she see that?

He clenched his fists at his sides to stop himself from grabbing her slender shoulders and making her look at him, and looked at her instead, seeing how different she was now. He missed the female who had stood up to him countless times and had put him in his place. That woman seemed to have disappeared that fateful night when he had recognised her as his fated female but hadn't been given a chance to tell her. She had been ripped from his grasp when he had been forced to take his place in the pride upon his father's death, picking up his mantle.

As alpha.

Cavanaugh felt as if he had lost her then and his heart had fractured. She had drifted away from him, always leaving when the females of status within the pride approached him, even when he had yearned for her to stay.

He had ached for her to look at him and smile, and let him know that she was okay.

He hadn't wanted the attention from the females. He had wanted hers. He had wanted them, as they should have been, together.

He had craved her.

Still craved her.

"Why are you here?" he whispered, still aching for her to look at him and smile, and let him know that she was okay.

He ached to hear her voice again and hear her tell him that she had come for him. He needed her to put him out of his misery. He needed her to tell him that nothing had changed between them despite everything that had happened and that there was a chance for him. He needed it as he had never needed anything before, as if it was as vital as air in his lungs or a beat in his chest. She had power over him as no other did. Not even the male who had come close to defeating him could contend with her.

She had the power to crush him, to kill him.

And she did it with only a handful of words.

"Please come back to the pride."

Those words struck his already aching heart like daggers, each one sending pain blazing outwards from the centre of his chest.

She hadn't come for him because she had wanted to be with him. He had been a fool to allow his heart to convince him that she'd had the courage he had lacked and had come to wait out the days with him until they could be together again.

She was here on pride business.

"You came all this way to ask me that?" He frowned at her, his tone flat and as empty as he felt inside as everything sank in. Nothing had changed. Five years of hell followed by five years of torture, and they still had a wall between them, a barrier that seemed impenetrable. He wanted to tear it down, but it was intangible, constructed of tradition and rules that went back millennia, laws that were so ingrained in them that they couldn't break free and were slaves to them. "I left the pride, Eloise. I have no interest in returning to it. I have no reason to go back there. The pride doesn't need me. It has an alpha."

"The pride needs you." She lifted her head a fraction and he thought she might look him in the eye and put a little fire behind her words, but she remained meek and polite.

The way a female of her status should speak to her alpha.

He growled and stalked towards her, and she backed away, turning more submissive as she wrapped her arms around herself.

"The pride doesn't need me." He stopped short of saying that she did though, and he needed her. He reached out to seize her arm but she flinched away, stopping him in his tracks. He softened and looked at her, seeing a broken and hurt female, not the strong and confident one she had been a decade ago. Fury filled him, burning fiercely in his veins, flooding him with a need to know what had happened to her. That need blazed in his heart, demanding that he ask her and make her answer him this time. "What the hell happened to you, Eloise? Who did this to you?"

She swallowed hard and finally looked up at him, right into his eyes, but still refused to tell him. "The pride needs you. You're the strongest male and our alpha. Please. Return with me."

"I told you. I'm not interested in returning." He wanted to reach out and smooth his hand along the soft curve of her jaw to keep her golden-brown eyes on him, but he didn't have the heart when she looked as if it was taking her great effort not to lower her gaze again.

"I travelled two years to find you... to bring you back to the pride."

He wished she had stopped at the first part, where she had only travelled two years to find him.

The pain in her eyes increased, her fear a palpable thing now that hung in the air between them, and it forced him to listen. What had happened at the pride? Concern for his village grew in his heart but concern for Eloise overshadowed it, pulling the focus of his thoughts back to her.

She must have searched for him across Bhutan, India and Europe, no doubt flashing his photograph to any fae or demon she came across. What terrible thing had happened to drive her to such a desperate and dangerous act?

Had she gained her scars during her search for him? Had some of the fae or demons captured her and held her for some nefarious reason?

He growled again, unable to contain it as he pictured her bound and afraid. His claws grew, emerging as he thought about hunting down whoever had hurt her and tearing into them. He wanted their blood on his hands. The scent of Eloise's fear grew stronger and he pulled down a deep breath to steady himself, not wanting to frighten her with his anger.

Cavanaugh looked her over again, self-reproach burning through him as her voice ran around his head, taunting him.

Two years.

Her journey would have been a difficult one, and not only because she had never left their homeland and had no experience of the world. Her position in the pride meant she had very little money, only a small allowance that he knew she had been saving her entire life. It wouldn't have been enough to cover luxuries like flights and hotels or even restaurants.

Her tattered clothing, her fatigue and how much weight she had lost since the last time he had seen her all confirmed his worst fears. She had spent two years living rough, sleeping on the streets or in hostels and travelling by foot, by hitchhiking or by jumping trains.

The thought of his little female living in such a fashion, day-to-day, probably stealing food and fearing for her safety, cut him right down to his soul and had his heart burning with a need to gather her into his arms and somehow take away every terrible experience she must have had.

It was his fault.

He had ventured far from the mountains and the pride village. If he hadn't left Bhutan, she could have easily found him. She wouldn't have been forced to spend years travelling and tracking him down.

If he had gone back for her—no, he couldn't think like that. He had warred with himself at the time about it and it had played on his mind ever since.

It had been too dangerous.

He had fought Stellan countless times and had always driven the male back into submission.

Except the last time.

That time he had allowed the male to defeat him.

It had only taken a passing thought during their fight, a split-second in which Cavanaugh had realised that he could be free of his position as alpha and could change the course of his life for the better, towards how he wanted it to be, by using the five year rule if he lost the fight but survived.

In that moment, Stellan had dealt what would have been a killing blow if the male hadn't slipped on the icy ground. The pain had been so intense that it had blinded Cavanaugh, forcing him to shift back from his snow leopard form. When he had seen all the blood on him and the deep wounds on his chest, he had feared he wouldn't survive to claim Eloise and the future he wanted with her.

His snow leopard side had still been partially in control, muddled in with his human mind because of the pain, and it had responded to that deep need. It had seized control and forced him to flee the village and venture high into the mountains to lick his wounds.

Days had passed before his deeper animal instincts had receded and he had realised with dismay what he had done.

He hadn't intended to lose the fight. He hadn't intended to leave Eloise behind. But both of those things had happened and there had been nothing he could do to change them.

Stellan had locked down the village and would have killed him if he had tried to return for Eloise.

Cavanaugh had waited almost a week to see whether she might leave, straying far enough from the village boundaries for him to reach her. She hadn't and he had been growing weaker, the cold slowing his healing and stealing his strength. He had been forced to head down the mountain.

Once there, he had come to the hard decision to leave Bhutan and wait for the five years to pass so he could give Eloise the life that she deserved.

To give her that life, he needed to be free of his position.

So he had convinced himself that she was better off at the pride, safe there until the five years were up and he could return to her and try to win her heart.

But the pain in her haunted eyes said that he had been wrong. He had left her at the pride and she had paid for it in ways she didn't want to speak about, ones that had broken her spirit. His instincts as her fated male and his heart pressed him to make her tell him what had happened to her. He needed to know.

"Eloise…" He wasn't sure what he could say to make everything better. There was nothing he could say. She had braved the world, and every danger imaginable, in order to find him. Whatever had happened at the pride, it had been bad to drive her to leave and seek him out. He looked at her wrists again and couldn't stop himself from pressing her, because he suddenly felt sure those scars hadn't happened during her journey and it left him sick to his stomach. "What happened?"

"It doesn't matter. Please. You must return to the pride."

It damn well did matter. He could order her to tell him, but he didn't want things to be that way between them. She wasn't beneath him. She was above him, deserved to be worshipped by him as her fated male.

"Please come back. The pride needs you."

He didn't like the restrained way she argued with him. There was a time when she would have playfully hit him and given him a piece of her mind. Maybe she would in eight days.

In eight days, things could begin to return to how he had liked them and he could forget the last five years, and the five that had come before them.

Could he convince her to wait? Could he delay her long enough for those days to pass? Gods, he wished that he could, even when the steely edge to her gaze said that he couldn't.

She had a reason for hunting him down and asking him to come back, and the piece of his heart that still cared about his pride said to listen to it, even when the rest warned it would end in misery for him. He would be throwing away the five years he had spent living with his regrets, looking forward to the day he could finally correct all his mistakes and make something good come out of them.

What if he told her that she was his fated female?

As soon as he thought that, he shoved it away. He couldn't. Not yet. At this point, it would only hurt her, just as it would have hurt her if he had told her after he had assumed the role of alpha all those years ago. They couldn't be together as mates yet and that meant he had to wait. Once he was free of his position, he would break the news to her somehow.

But for that to happen, he needed to stay away from the village until the five years were up.

"Stay a while and we'll talk about everything. You need to rest and eat. You're worn out and I can see it," he said and he swore her eyes had flashed fire at him.

She was on to him. She knew he was out to stall her.

Her eyes darkened.

"We don't have time. The pride doesn't have time. I have to take you back to the village now," she said, her voice gaining confidence and fire at last. "I have to go back."

It seemed she had been counting the days since he had left just as he had.

"Why?" He frowned at the resolve that burned in her words. This was important to her, perhaps more so than he had thought, and he began to get the sinking feeling that something had gone terribly wrong back at the pride, something he wouldn't be able to ignore, not even for eight days. "Eloise... if you really want me to go back, you need to tell me why you left."

"I did it because I knew I could find you... because I had hoped that I could convince you to do the right thing," she snapped and glared at him, anger lacing her scent, frustration and disappointment that he could feel in her. "Your kin are living in a dictatorship... Stellan is a tyrant... many of us have been killed and the rest of us..."

Her voice faded and she wrapped her arms around herself, lowered her head and clutched the sleeves of her grey coat, bunching the material into her trembling fists.

"I am sorry. I shouldn't have spoken to you like that," she whispered.

13

He wasn't sorry. She had given him hope that the woman he had known a decade ago still existed inside her and that he could have that woman back in his life. Everything could return to how it had been.

But it couldn't at the same time.

The thought of his pride being mistreated, abused, and murdered sat like a block of ice in his chest. He couldn't ignore what had happened. He had to do something about it. Before becoming their alpha, he had been their strongest male. Eloise knew that and she had risked her life to travel across the world in search of him, to bring him back to the pride and restore peace at the village.

She wanted him to free them from the tyranny of the male he had left as their leader. He could see how important it was to her and that made it even more important to him.

He would do something about it, but he was damned if he was going to set foot in the village until the eight days were up. Once he was free of his status, Stellan would be the alpha and he would be just a challenger for that title. He could take down Stellan and pass on the position, remaining free of the pride rules.

He needed to find a way to stall her.

Eight days were all that stood between him and claiming the mate he craved with all of his heart.

Those eight days suddenly felt like forever.

He had the dreadful feeling that the woman he loved was about to be snatched from his grasp again.

CHAPTER 3

Eloise stood in an expansive pale-walled room in the presence of her alpha, fighting to stop herself from looking at him and drinking in the sight of him as she wanted to. She had thought that she would be ready to see Cavanaugh again when she had heard that he worked at this nightclub in the heart of London.

She had been wrong.

He was as handsome as she remembered, maybe even more so now. The angular strong line of his cut jaw framed a face with intense stormy eyes and sculpted cheekbones, and the most profane mouth she had ever seen on a male. His sensual lips curved wickedly beneath his straight nose. The sight of him had her heart pounding and her palms sweating, and she had to keep reminding herself that he was the alpha of their pride.

A male far above her now.

He had been her friend once. Her best friend.

He had been more than that too.

They had been close for her entire life, and nearly eighty years into that friendship, around a decade ago, they had become more than friends. He had started visiting more often and had started looking at her differently, with hungry eyes that had awakened the true depths of her feelings for him.

She had been deeply aware of him whenever he had been around her, every stolen glance and smile, every innocent brush of their bodies. He had been approaching one hundred, the time of sexual maturity for snow leopard shifters, and she had known it was affecting him, because being around him had affected her. It had lured her to him and she had been powerless to resist.

Like a moth drawn to a flame, it hadn't ended well for her.

She wasn't sure now that it had ended well for him either.

She had been angry when he had left, but she had understood his motivation for doing it. He had tired of the constant fight to hold on to the pride.

Stellan had returned three years into Cavanaugh's reign as alpha and had constantly challenged him. They had come to blows several times but Cavanaugh had always won, and the battles had never been as drawn out and brutal as the night Stellan had driven Cavanaugh from the pride.

Cavanaugh hadn't returned, and even though it had hurt her, she understood why he had remained away. He had thought the pride was in better hands, but he was wrong.

His gaze bore into her but she kept her eyes on her worn boots.

They were about to fall apart. She felt as if she might join them. She was weary, bone-deep tired. All she really wanted to do was curl up somewhere and sleep, to rest as he had offered. It would be nice to sleep somewhere safe for once, without having to try to rest with one part of her alert and ready for anything.

She couldn't stop now though. She had been scouring the world for him for two years, driven by a need to find him and bring him back to the pride. Her promise had kept her going through every cold night when she had been too afraid to sleep and every day when she had been so hungry she had wanted to cry.

Her promise and the thought of seeing him again.

The moment she had set eyes on him, standing behind the bar of the nightclub, his white shirt and wild silver hair making him stand out beneath the coloured lights, all of her strength had disappeared.

She had found herself on the brink of collapse, suddenly aware of how tired, hungry and weak she was.

Suddenly, painfully, aware of everything she had been through since leaving the pride, and everything that she had endured before that, when she had been in the village.

She wanted to give in to him and collapse into his arms and let him be strong for her, ached with a need to feel them around her and breathe him in, to feel him against her and know that he was real. It really was Cavanaugh standing before her, looking at her with concern in his beautiful stormy eyes.

She needed him to hold her and hold her together at the same time until she had found her feet.

But she couldn't.

She was weak right now and she wouldn't be able to find the strength to place the necessary distance between them again.

She had to hold herself back and deny the deep needs running through her.

She wasn't here for only her sake and she had to remember that. People were counting on her to bring Cavanaugh back to the pride. She had promised the others that she would. She had sworn that she knew him well enough that she could find him, and she had. They believed in her, were depending on her and on Cavanaugh, and she wouldn't fail them, even though part of her didn't want him to return to the role of alpha.

She had missed him.

She had been missing him for ten years.

She had thought about leaving the pride to find him before, but her mother had been there. Her friends too. Leaving had been a frightening prospect, until Stellan had begun abusing his rights and had announced his plans. Then, staying had become frightening and leaving had been her only hope of helping her kin, and saving herself.

Eloise risked a glance at Cavanaugh. He smiled at her and she realised that he was more handsome now. She hadn't seen him smile like that, the warmth of it filling his dark grey eyes, for almost a decade. It made her feel awful. He had found his smile again in this place, far from their homeland and free from the pride and the struggles of being an alpha.

Here she was trying to force him to come back with her, when he was close to being free of his position.

His attempts to delay her had confirmed her suspicions.

Pride rules stated that if an alpha remained out of the boundaries of the village for five years, their role would pass to another. Stellan had challenged Cavanaugh, had defeated him, but had failed to kill him. Cavanaugh still held the status of pride alpha. Stellan could only call himself their alpha, and he had ensured no one would dare stand up to him by killing the first three males who had tried.

"Will you return with me?" she said, needing an answer, because she was wasting precious time.

After discovering where he was, she had checked the flights out of London in an internet café. There was a flight tomorrow to New Delhi that would connect with a flight to Paro International Airport in Bhutan.

They needed to be on those flights.

She hated what she was doing, but she didn't want Cavanaugh to fight. She needed to convince him to come with her now and not allow him to delay her. The part of her that didn't want to hurt him by forcing him to return to the pride before it passed to Stellan warred with the part that couldn't bear the thought of seeing him fight again. If Stellan became the alpha, Cavanaugh would have to fight and kill Stellan to free the pride from his tyranny.

If she could convince Cavanaugh to return now, while he was still their alpha, Stellan would have to stand down because Cavanaugh would have the entire pride on his side.

"I will go back with you," he said and relief beat through her, lasting only as long as it took for him to speak again. "I have a few things I have to tie up here, and I need to get leave to go. You can stay here while I take care of them and maybe I can show you around London? You've always wanted to see it."

Her hope faded again and she frowned down at her boots, fighting the anger rising swiftly within her. He was stalling her. He meant to make her wait until the five years were up and then he would have to fight. Her gut clenched, churning as she thought about him locked in battle with Stellan, and her blood turned to ice but burned like an inferno at the same time. Every instinct she possessed, every feeling she had for him, demanded she keep pushing him until he agreed to go back with her.

"It'll be like old times." Those five words were a temptation that she found difficult to resist.

She wanted things to be like old times, but she couldn't have it happen at the expense of the pride and everyone waiting for her.

For him.

She couldn't have it happen at the expense of Cavanaugh's safety.

The thought of him fighting turned her stomach over again and she fought the memories that bombarded her, a bloody replay of his last battle against Stellan.

She had to make him listen to her, and make him understand what was happening, and that meant she had to tell him something that she had hoped to avoid mentioning. She didn't want to hurt him by telling him everything that had been happening, because she knew he would feel responsible, but she could no longer avoid it. Her only chance of convincing him to leave on the next available flight was to say things straight, no matter how much they hurt him.

"I'm going without you then." She spoke to her boots at first, but the fire burning in her veins became too hot for her to deny and she lifted her head and looked him in the eye, because she needed to see her words striking their mark and know he would save the pride. "Cavanaugh... your pride needs you... if you don't return... he has been making full use of the pride rules. When he ascends to the role of alpha, when you hand it to him, he intends to take every unmated female in the pride, whether they are willing or not."

His dark stormy eyes slowly widened and then narrowed, his silver-white eyebrows dropping low above them.

"Including me." She looked away from him when he snarled, baring sharp fangs, and the centres of his irises turned silver.

She closed her eyes.

"If you don't help me... I'm not sure what will happen to me or the others."

His hands clamped down on her shoulders, his grip firm and speaking of his strength, and she wanted to step into his arms and have him hold her again, as he used to, back before her entire world had crumbled around her.

"Eloise," he husked and she refused to look at him.

She couldn't when her mind was locked on the things that Stellan had in store for her and the other females, things that made her skin crawl and made her want to do something drastic.

Something terrible.

Taking her own life would be favourable over having that vile male touching her and using her body against her will.

"Eloise?" Cavanaugh's deep voice curled around her, the warmth of it chasing back her dark thoughts, and she tensed as he tried to draw her into his arms.

She couldn't.

No matter how much she wanted to be in them.

He growled, released her and paced away. She opened her eyes and tracked him as he took swift strides across the concrete floor, scrubbing his hand over the soft spikes of his silver-white hair. Silver shone in his eyes as he muttered to himself, his agitation clear to her in his scent.

"Please, Cavanaugh… it has to be now."

He stopped and looked across at her, a myriad of emotions playing out in his grey eyes, feelings that conflicted and collided with each other. She was tearing him apart with what she was asking, and she hated herself for it, but she couldn't leave the other females and the pride to fend for itself. She never wanted to cause him pain, because it hurt her too, made her ache when she saw it in his eyes, but she couldn't give up until he had agreed and they were heading for Bhutan.

"Wait here," he said and strode back towards the door they had entered through.

Where was he going?

She debated it and then disobeyed him, bending his order a little to accommodate her curiosity. She would remain in the room, interpreting it as the here he had mentioned. He yanked the door open and she caught it before it closed and scanned the dark club for him. The music was obnoxiously loud and the colourful lights blinded her. She couldn't understand how he could work in this place, but he did seem to like it here.

This place had become his home.

She spotted him directly to her left, talking to the sandy-haired male behind the bar. They were almost the same height, and wore the same white shirt with their trousers, but the other male seemed gloomy. He slid his golden eyes towards her and said something to Cavanaugh. Cavanaugh looked back at her over his wide shoulders and huffed.

She ducked back into the room where she was meant to be waiting. What was he doing? Gaining permission to leave? It seemed odd that he had to do such a thing. He was a pride alpha, but here he was nothing more than serving staff.

Was this the sort of life he had wanted for himself?

He had always seemed happiest during the years when his father had ruled and he'd had few responsibilities. He had been as happy with that simple life as she had been.

She could see the appeal of this place for him. Serving people drinks. Meeting people. Exchanging stories. He had little responsibility here. It was a world away from the pride village and his life there.

It took her back to those happier years they had shared, when all they had done was complete their tasks for the day before meeting up and hiking in the mountains, climbing, or just lazing by the fire and talking about the world beyond the village.

She had loved those days the most, when the snow swirled thickly outside the windows of his home and he had laid close to her on the furs in front of his fireplace, his back against the couch, his grey eyes filled with light and a sparkle as he recounted his tales of his travels. He had smiled constantly, but there had been times when he had looked into her eyes and it had faded, and she had been deeply aware of him.

As a male.

A beautiful and powerful man.

She closed her eyes and could almost smell the smoke of the fire. She could almost hear the rich timbre of his laughter whenever she had leaned closer to him, amusing him with her eagerness to hear more about the places he had been. She could almost feel the intensity of his gaze during those times when they would both fall silent and look into each other's eyes, the world around them dropping away.

She could almost feel the soft whisper of his fingers across her cheek and the electric thrill of the first time his lips had brushed hers.

The door opened again, a brief blast of noise assaulting her just as she had grown used to the muted sounds of the club beyond the thick door. She turned on her heel to face Cavanaugh, a wave of heat scalding her cheeks and heart pounding from the sudden intrusion into her fantasy and the sight of him standing before her.

A dangerously alluring male.

One who made her want to forget all her pain and her sorrow, shed all of the bad memories and cling to the good ones, and step into his arms and surrender to him.

Eloise trembled on the brink, filled with a need to give in to temptation. His grey gaze narrowed on her, a curious but confused edge to it. She managed to drag her eyes away from him before he could figure her out and see through her to the conflict that raged inside her.

He huffed and shoved his fingers through his silver-white hair again.

"All set. Come on." He grabbed her hand before she could protest, pulling her along behind him.

His hand was warm on hers. Big. It easily encompassed her one, making her feel small and a little weak, even though she was far from that. He had told her countless times that she was a strong female.

It had made her believe that she was one worthy of him.

She shoved that memory aside and followed him up a metal staircase to another floor. He pushed open the first dark wooden door in the long corridor and held it for her. She passed him, her gaze taking in the small blue bedroom.

He had somehow managed to squeeze a double bed into the space on her left, but it hadn't left much room for his other furniture. Against the wall to her right stood a wardrobe, a chest of drawers and then another door. The gap between the furniture and the bed was so narrow that Cavanaugh had to shuffle sideways through it to reach the small space in front of that door.

He stopped there, began unbuttoning his white shirt and had pulled it off over his head before she could look away. Her mouth went dry as she stared at his back and his powerful arms. He had always had a fine physique but it was even more breathtaking now, muscular and defined, speaking to the most feminine part of her that purred in appreciation of his masculinity before she could get control over it.

He tossed the shirt into an overflowing basket in the corner of the room beside him, paused and suddenly frowned over his bare shoulder at her. She pinned her eyes on the dark blue covers of the bed and fought to stifle the blush that burned up her cheeks. What the hell was she doing? Besides setting herself up for another broken heart.

"Sit." He jerked his chin towards the bed and she obeyed, perching on the edge of the mattress opposite the wardrobe. "I'll grab some stuff and hit the shower, and you can use it after me."

"There's a flight tomorrow for New Delhi. It will get us there in time for the connecting flight." Talking business seemed like the best way to get her mind off the fact that he was half-naked and tempting her all over again. She couldn't give in. No matter how much she wanted to surrender to the desire for him that had never died.

He paused in the doorway to what she presumed was the bathroom and looked back at her, his cheeks a little paler than she remembered. "We're flying into Paro?"

She nodded and almost smiled when he grabbed the doorframe to steady himself. She had forgotten how little he liked the only international airport in Bhutan. Apparently, landings and take-offs were often a rather hair-raising affair. The strip was short and surrounded by mountains on all sides. He had told her about it countless times, whenever he had returned from a trip outside of the country, but she had never seen it herself. She had used the roads to cross over into India when she had come looking for him.

He shuddered and disappeared into the bathroom.

Eloise stared at the door he had left open when the shower switched on, extremely aware of where she was—in his room, on his bed.

Alone with him.

Her heart pounded, her awareness of him increasing as she heard the rustle of his clothes hitting the floor. She idly stroked her hands over the bed covers, unable to stop herself as she listened to him. His scent was strong on them, encompassing her. Weakening her. It filled her senses, a touch of wood smoke, snow and spice. She had missed that smell. She drew a deep breath of it, pulling it over her teeth to savour it, and closed her eyes as she listened to him showering.

Each sudden splash of water had her imagining how it would sluice off his powerful body, cascading over his honed muscles, rippling down every peak and valley of his torso, and his back. She shivered and heated inside, losing herself in fantasising about him, the world around her fading away once more.

Only the feel of his gaze on her brought her crashing back to Earth.

Her eyes shot open, immediately leaping straight to him where he stood in the doorway, a white towel slung around his waist, riding low on his lean hips. Her gaze drank in the delicious sight of his naked torso and her cheeks heated as she swiftly directed it back to the floor.

He heaved a sigh and she screwed her eyes shut and tried not to picture him walking around the room, moving so close to her that they almost touched as he pulled items from his wardrobe. What was she doing? He had broken her heart once already.

No. He had broken it a thousand times.

It had broken every day that she'd had to watch him as the pride's alpha, witnessing the way all the women of status fawned over him, and how he didn't turn them away.

It had broken every time he hadn't looked at her when she had found the courage to look at him.

It had shattered completely when he had disappeared into the night, leaving her afraid that he would die from his injuries somewhere or she would never see him again.

The journey to find him had been long and treacherous, but she had a feeling that the short journey back to the pride would feel a hundred times longer and a million times more dangerous.

Here, she felt as if she was in a different world. Was this how he felt? Did he feel that here the rules didn't exist? Did he feel as free as they had been once, long ago?

It was already a struggle to remember that he was the pride alpha and she was a female without standing, one far beneath him.

She wasn't sure how she was going to survive the next eight days with him, resisting the old feelings that were coming back to life inside her.

She had to do it though, even if it pained her.

Even though she knew that each step she took that brought them closer to the pride was a step further away from what she truly wanted.

It was a step further away from having him.

CHAPTER 4

Cavanaugh tossed all the gear he had bought into the open back of the battered Jeep Wrangler he had purchased from a local at a very steep price. He didn't care about how it looked as long as it survived the run up to the end of the dirt track where their trek through the forest would begin, and back again. He walked around to the driver's side of the black vehicle, opened the door and pulled himself up onto the seat.

Eloise looked across at him and he handed her the plastic bag with the gear he had bought for her in it. She took it and peered into the bag. It wasn't much, just a lightweight dark grey fleece and a pair of beige trekking trousers, but it managed to get a smile out of her. He couldn't wait to see her face when she saw the pair of boots he had placed into the back of the vehicle. He hadn't failed to notice hers were on their last legs.

He turned on the engine, clicked his seatbelt into place and pulled out onto the quiet road.

The drive was long, taking several hours just to reach the end of the paved road where it gave way to little more than a mud track. The scenery was stunning though, on display all around him in the open top Jeep, and Eloise seemed intent on taking it in, avoiding looking at him.

He stared ahead of him, towards the distant snow-capped mountains that protected their village, his mind running back over everything that Eloise had told him.

Cavanaugh flexed his fingers around the steering wheel and glared at the mountains, part of him itching to reach them and Stellan. The male was going to pay for the things he had done, and for the disgusting things he had planned too. Cavanaugh had tried to shed the sense of responsibility he felt for the pride, but as the oldest son of his father, he'd had it beaten into him since birth.

When Eloise had announced her intention to leave with or without him, she had known what she was doing. She had made it impossible for him to do anything other than go with her. He hadn't been able to let her return alone, knowing what awaited her. He hadn't been able to delay her either, knowing what would happen to his kin if he did.

He had spent the entirety of the two plane journeys, including the dangerous landing into Paro airport, thinking about what she was asking him to do and planning it all out. He had no interest in being the alpha. The one thing he had craved in his life wasn't power or standing. It was her. She was the only thing that mattered to him.

This journey was his chance to convince her that she was his mate.

His plan was simple. He intended to let the remaining days pass somehow so he entered the village as a free man. He would straighten everything out with Eloise, do right by his kin as their strongest male by eliminating Stellan, and then he would go back to Underworld.

Hopefully with her.

It sounded simple anyway. He had a feeling that it was going to be anything but that.

It was late afternoon by the time they reached the end of the mud track. Cavanaugh parked the vehicle on the side of the road, turned off the engine and stepped out. Eloise opened the passenger side door and stepped down onto the mud, muttering something to herself. He rounded the back of the vehicle, pulled out the cardboard box that contained the trekking boots he had bought for her, and held it out to her. She eyed it with surprise and then smiled when she opened it.

"You can't trek through the forest in those," he said with a smile in the direction of her old boots and she nodded.

"Thank you." She toed off her boots one by one and he somehow found the strength to turn his back to give her some privacy as she changed into her new clothes.

Cavanaugh busied himself with putting everything he had purchased into their backpacks. He had ensured they had everything they needed, from a canteen to climbing ropes and harnesses, to a GPS. He had even purchased protein bars. As much as he hated them, they were a necessity. They couldn't hunt during the trek and both of them needed to keep their strength up.

Eloise rounded the back of the vehicle and took the pack he handed her, slipping it onto her shoulders. She tugged the straps to get it comfortable while he put on his own larger pack. He pocketed the keys to the vehicle and set off, following the narrow path that led from the end of the dirt road down into the forest.

They had walked for almost half a mile before Cavanaugh gave in to the constant unsettling feeling in his gut and stepped to one side on the track to allow Eloise past him. He didn't like her walking behind him where he couldn't keep an eye on her and make sure that she was safe. She looked at him, slowing her approach and he jerked his chin to his left, silently telling her to take the lead. His gaze raked over her as she walked past him, taking in every inch of her.

She looked better now, less haunted and had more colour, but she still barely resembled the woman he had left five years ago.

He had insisted on feeding her up, despite her protests, ensuring she'd had a good breakfast at Underworld before taking a nap there. At the airport in London, he had managed to get her to eat a large dinner with him, and then a further meal when they had reached New Delhi. He had even convinced her to sleep on the planes. She had surprised him by sleeping through the landing in Paro and he had been loath to wake her when they'd had to disembark. How long had it been since she had gotten some good sleep?

She still looked as if she needed about a week of it.

Maybe offering her a sightseeing trip around London had been the wrong approach when he had been attempting to stall her. He should have offered her his bed for a week of uninterrupted sleep.

Cavanaugh followed her through the forest, his gaze locked on her, taking in her curves beneath her dark grey fleece and her beige trousers. The more he studied her, the fiercer he burned with a need to step up behind her, place his hands on her hips, and draw her back against him. He wanted to hold her, and feel her in his arms, back with him again.

Safe with him.

Safe.

That single word sent his mind down darker paths. The thought that Stellan might have already hurt her, might be responsible for the scarring on her wrists, drove him mad with a need to track the bastard down and beat him into a bloody pulp. But Stellan wasn't the only one to blame. No matter how much he wanted to pin it all on the other male, most of the blame for what Eloise had been through rested on his own shoulders.

Terrible things had happened to her because he had left the pride. The mistakes he had made had resulted in her being hurt. It sat in his stomach like a lead weight, dragging him down. He wanted to ask her again what had happened to her, but he feared he wouldn't be strong enough to hear her answer.

He wanted to apologise to her, but he wasn't sure what to say. Nothing he said could erase what she had been through. He had to try though.

"Eloise," he started and faltered when she looked back at him, her honey-coloured eyes bright in the evening light and wide with curiosity. He scrubbed the back of his neck with his left hand and his courage failed him. "Nothing."

A frown flickered on her brow and she looked as if she might question him, and then she turned away from him again, giving him a view of her backside that proved to be just the distraction he needed from his dark thoughts.

She began up an incline and banked left, following a trail that tracked the river to her right.

Cavanaugh looked up through the trees, checking the light level. It had taken most of the day to find a vehicle, purchase all the equipment they needed, and drive the seven hours up the track. In just over an hour, it would be dark. They would have to stop and make camp. Near to the river would be the best place to set up the small tent he had purchased and start a fire, but also the most dangerous. Countless predators made the forest their home, big cats among them, and many of them hunted along the water where their prey would come to drink.

He could smell them in the area. Tigers. Leopards. Even clouded leopards. None of them would take well to him and Eloise being in their territory. The tigers were the biggest threat. They had been known to take human prey in the past, when times had been tough for them, and had spread their territory far and wide, even up to altitude in places, clashing with the territory of the snow leopards.

The trail ended two miles deeper into the forest, at a large pool that glittered at the base of a short waterfall. This was as far as the locals went, coming here to try their luck fishing. He had met a few once, years ago, on his way down from the mountain. They hadn't seemed surprised to see someone coming from a direction where nature prevailed and no humans ventured. He suspected that the legends the locals believed in were based on his pride and those legends were woven deep into their traditions and religion. They had known what he was, but they respected him and his kind.

Eloise distracted him from his memories by clambering up the enormous boulders that formed a wall ahead of him. He stared at her backside, cupped tightly in her trekking trousers. He might have purchased a size smaller than he should have, but he had known she wouldn't dare complain about how tight and revealing they were. It was the first time he felt that being an alpha was a perk, not a punishment.

She leaped to another boulder and scaled the next one with ease.

Snow leopard shifters were agile climbers in both of their forms, and he had always loved climbing with her, scaling the dangerous mountains that surrounded the village in the hidden valley high above this forest. There were ledges on the mountains that offered the most incredible and breathtaking views across the Himalayas.

Her boot slipped and he was behind her in a single leap, his hands pressed against her backside to stop her from falling. She gasped and turned wide honey-coloured eyes on him, a blush climbing her cheeks before she recovered and stole her body from his grasp, ruining the moment. She hauled herself back towards the rocks and up them, away from his hands.

Hands that ached to touch her again, to explore every inch of her at his leisure, together with his lips.

"Damned new boots," she muttered and was more careful as she clambered up the rocks, placing each foot with caution.

When she had reached the top, she looked back down at him. He grinned and ascended the treacherous rocks in a few leaps, using his superior strength and agility to make easy work of it. She huffed under her breath and stalked on ahead of him, evidently not impressed by his display of manliness.

Cavanaugh shrugged and followed her, his senses split between her and their surroundings now that they were heading deeper into the forest, away from the farmland and the humans.

He closed the distance between them as the terrain turned hilly, the ascents and descents steep and muddy, making it tough going as they continued to track the river through the forest covering the valley. He helped her as much as she would let him, growing increasingly frustrated whenever she refused to accept his assistance. Back in the day, she had never hesitated to take his hand when he had offered it or his help whenever she had slipped. Was it because she could only see him as her pride's alpha now?

He wasn't that male, not when he was with her.

He was just Cavanaugh.

The air grew humid as they followed the river. The evening light danced across its rippling surface, making it look like liquid gold. He drew in a deep breath, catching the scents of the animals and all the different plants and trees, refreshing his memory of this place he had called home for a century.

It was beautiful, but tarnished now.

His reason for being here, and everything that had happened, had ruined it for him, stealing something away from the stunning scenery. The mountains called to him, rising high above the forest that surrounded him, their snow-capped peaks piercing the golden sky, but he no longer felt the deep need to answer that call, to rush up to their pinnacles and see the world as they did.

He was happier down here, in the forest.

Truthfully, he was happier miles away from this place that no longer felt like his home.

Eloise looked back at him, the sight of her soothing him and chasing away his heavy thoughts.

The forest drew back from the river ahead of them, leaving a wide earth bank on their side that gave way to pebbles and then rounded stones by the water.

"We can camp ahead." Cavanaugh scanned the forest with his senses. "I've camped here a few times."

It smelled different now though. The territories of the cats that made this area their home had shifted.

Movement across the river caught his eye and his gaze snapped there, his senses on high alert. A small leopard cat broke cover, spotted him and dashed back into the scrub. They weren't much bigger than a domestic cat and were definitely not a threat to him and Eloise.

She set her backpack down in the middle of the dirt bank and rubbed her shoulders. He would do that for her if she asked. Gods, he would do it for her if she didn't ask. He would do anything to get his hands back on her and break down the damned wall that stood between them. He dumped his backpack and stretched, a sliver of pleasure flowing through him as he loosened up. He wasn't looking forward to the ascent ahead of him, not with so much gear. He would have to stash most of it somewhere rather than trying to carry it up the mountain path.

His gaze drifted along the wide slow river, hopping from boulder to boulder that dotted the water, and then up over the trees to the mountains in the distance ahead of him.

He was running out of time.

There had to be a way to get Eloise to look at him and see him as the man she had known all her life, the one who belonged to her if she would have him, and not her alpha.

He sighed and set the tent up as he pondered that, and then left her to handle the fire as he looked at the river. It had been a hard trek and he needed to wash up before settling down to a delicious meal of protein bars. The crystal clear water was just too inviting to resist.

He wanted to cool off with a swim.

If all went to plan, Eloise would join him.

CHAPTER 5

"I'm going for a swim."

Eloise barely had time to register those words before Cavanaugh was stripping off his charcoal fleece, tugging the dark t-shirt he wore beneath off with it too. He dropped them on top of his pack and she stared at him, unable to drag her eyes away as they slowly glided down over the hard slabs of his pectorals to the ropes of his stomach.

An ache started low in her belly and only got worse as he tugged off his walking boots, pulled off his socks, and unbuttoned his dark grey trousers. He pushed them down, revealing long toned legs, and stepped out of them, his muscles shifting with the action, mesmerising her.

He truly was a majestic male.

For a moment, she feared he would crush her strength to resist him by stripping completely, but he turned away from her, his black trunks still in place. They hugged the twin globes of his backside as he walked and she stared at them, loving the way they dimpled and flexed with each stride he took towards the water.

When he looked back at her, she dropped her gaze to her pack.

She felt his eyes leave her and lifted hers back to him, drinking in the sight of him. He waded into the water and barked out a sharp noise that echoed around the lush green valley and the mountains beyond.

"Fuck, that's freezing." He didn't turn around as she had expected. He shuddered and kept wading out into the river, his shoulders hunched up and fingers flexing at his sides.

She smiled.

And hid it when he looked back at her.

He grinned, his grey eyes bright with it, a light she hadn't seen in them for a long time. Too long. This was the gorgeous male she had grown up with, always an air of mischief surrounding him, a sense that he was going to live his life to the fullest and take every adventure in his stride.

Seeing him like it again only made her feel worse about making him return to the pride with her and only made it hit home how much he had changed when he had become their alpha. She had never thought he would smile again as he was now, full of energy and happiness. She had never thought she would see the Cavanaugh who had been her best friend, her closest companion, and so much more than that.

For her at least.

She studied him, spotting all the changes that she had failed to notice, ones that were startlingly clear to her now and told her that things had been hard for Cavanaugh at the village after he had become their alpha. She could see now how much it had weighed on him and she cursed herself for being so wrapped up in her own hurt to notice his struggle. Her heart whispered that it wasn't only his duties as alpha that had made life at the pride hard for him and she tried to ignore it, afraid to listen to it and believe that his struggle had in part been because they had been separated and couldn't be together.

She refused to get caught up in that fantasy.

She refused to surrender to her pressing need to question him too, because she feared the answers he might give her.

He bravely dipped lower in the water, kicked off and began to swim in the deepest part of the river, entrancing her as he ducked his head under the cold water and surfaced again. He slicked his silver-white hair back and rivulets ran down his sculpted cheeks and rolled along the strong line of his jaw. He still made her heart beat hard and still drew her to him even though her memories of him were tainted by everything that had come afterwards.

The women.

The warmth that had been building inside her stuttered and died, leaving her ice cold.

Cavanaugh swam towards her, but his smile no longer affected her. The sight of him no longer made her want to rush into his arms and listen to his deep voice as he told her stories of the outside world. The pain of watching him from a distance for five long years crushed that need and the pain of being separated from him and everything she had endured destroyed her softer feelings.

"Join me, Eloise," he hollered, his smile widening. "It's not bad once you get used to it."

"No." That word came out far colder than she had intended and he frowned at her, his smile disappearing as he stopped swimming.

She looked away from him, unable to bear seeing the hurt as it crossed his face, tearing at her. She hadn't meant to reject him so cruelly. It had been wrong of her, and not because he was her alpha and she had been disrespectful. It had been wrong of her to hurt him when deep inside she had wanted to take him up on his offer.

She wanted to swim with him, but she couldn't shake the memories that were bombarding her, replays of the five years she had watched him from a distance as he had acted as their alpha.

She couldn't shake the flashes of the women who had been all over him, seeking his attention.

Eloise pressed her hands to her chest as her heart hurt and tears threatened to fill her eyes. She sniffed them back, unwilling to let them fall. She had spilled enough tears in her life over everything that had happened. She was done with them now. She was stronger than the woman she had been, the one shaped by events she'd had no control over.

The one who had been torn apart every night when Cavanaugh had gone to his house, a trail of women following him.

It was the right of pride alphas to take their pick from among the females of status, satisfying as many partners as took their fancy. The females vied for the attention of their alpha because sharing his bed might elevate them into the role of his sole female.

Cavanaugh had never chosen one from the many. His father had been like that too, bedding numerous females, never settling on one.

His father had even slept with the females without status, the ones who could never be selected as his sole female.

Her gaze sought Cavanaugh and tracked him as he swam away from her, the distance between them eating at her. How many females had he bedded in the five years he had served as their alpha?

How many more would he sleep with after he returned to that role?

He would return to it. He had no choice. He would become their true alpha again when he set foot in the village, and she would go back to her quiet life, away from the pride. As much as it hurt her, it was how things had to be. She wasn't bringing him back for her sake. She was doing it for the pride.

Eloise watched him, a deep need growing inside her again, one that she struggled to deny.

Asking Cavanaugh for the truth about how many women he had slept with and whether he had ever cared about her would only end with her being hurt again. She wasn't strong enough, wasn't brave enough to lay her heart on the line like that. Her stomach rebelled at the vision of him looking her right in the eye and telling her that he had bedded the females and that she had meant nothing to him, that what had happened between them had been nothing more than satisfying a biological need for him.

She wasn't strong enough right now to hear that. Seeing him again, speaking to him for the first time in almost a decade, and being close to him had her muddled and off balance, liable to fall apart and make a fool of herself.

Cavanaugh began swimming back towards her and the resolve she had mustered crumbled again. She trembled on the brink of casting aside all the rules and swimming with him. Part of her demanded she seized this moment with him, before he was taken from her again, but the rest warned that it would only make things worse. Giving herself to him again now would make seeing him with other females unbearable. The knowledge that he could again take something precious and special and treat it as if it was nothing would destroy her.

His gaze swung her way and his expression suddenly went cold.

"Eloise!" He shoved out of the water, spraying it everywhere and startling her.

He rushed across the wet rocks, his footing sure as he sprinted towards her, leaping with agile grace from one boulder to the next, his muscles working hard as he closed the distance between them.

Her eyes widened and she turned slowly, her heart thundering against her breast and cold prickles crawling over the nape of her neck.

She wasn't alone.

Her eyes met the huge tiger's ones as it stalked towards her from the edge of the forest, already close enough to pounce.

Her breath hitched and stuck in her throat.

Cavanaugh appeared between her and the tiger. His left hand clamped down on her waist and he pushed her behind him, shielding her with his big body.

He roared at the tiger and silver-grey fur rippled over his powerful shoulders.

His hand flexed against her hip, a silent warning to her, telling her not to move. She kept still, pulse racing at a dizzying pace, her blood running cold in her veins.

Beyond him, the tiger hunkered down, preparing to attack.

Eloise's heart leaped up to join her breath, lodging in her throat and refusing to come down. Fear blasted through her, the thought that Cavanaugh might have to fight the wild cat turning her blood to ice and filling her with a desperate need to do something in order to protect him. She was powerless though. No match for the beast. It wouldn't back down if she faced it. It would sense her weakness and attack.

Only Cavanaugh was strong enough to face the animal and make it leave.

The tiger growled, flashing long yellowing canines.

Cavanaugh snarled back at it. She could sense his desire to shift. It ran through her too, but it would be a grave mistake to give in to it. She was bigger in her human form and appeared far more like a threat to the tiger, and so was Cavanaugh. His hand trembled against her hip, cold from the water but filling her with comforting heat. Cavanaugh was strong. A king of beasts.

He could convince the tiger to leave them. She had to believe it, because she couldn't bear thinking about the other path things might take.

She couldn't think about Cavanaugh fighting.

It took her back five years, to a night she would never forget and one she didn't want to remember.

The sound of flesh striking flesh. The scent of blood on the cold air. The anguished bellow. The snow painted crimson. It all whirled in her mind, cranking up her fear, sending her heart into overdrive as she fought for air and to escape the nightmarish vision.

Cavanaugh's grip on her hip increased, driving away the gruesome vision but not her fear.

She stared up at the back of his head, fighting her need to touch him to reassure herself that he was fine and her need to do something to drive the beast away so he would remain that way.

He breathed hard, his eyes never leaving the tiger. The beast didn't take its eyes off Cavanaugh either. They stared at each other across the expanse of muddy rocky ground for what felt like hours to her, a silent standoff between two powerful predators. She couldn't take it. The air was too thick for her to breathe as she waited. She couldn't get it down into her lungs.

The tiger snarled.

Cavanaugh roared, the sound echoing around the forest and the mountains that rose above it.

Her heart stopped dead when the tiger went lower and she felt sure that it would pounce and Cavanaugh would have to fight it. She grabbed his arm, on the verge of pulling him out of danger.

The big cat turned and slinked back into the forest.

Her heart plunged into her stomach.

"Are you alri—"

Cavanaugh cut her off by turning on his heel and dragging her into his arms, against his damp chest. He wrapped his arms around her, steel bands that bordered on squeezing the air she had managed to get down into her lungs back out of them again.

She wasn't sure what to think when he pressed his cheek to the side of her head and cupped the back of it with one hand, tunnelling his fingers into the loose waves of her dark hair. She told herself not to do it, but ended up closing her eyes, pressing her hands to his stomach and resting her cheek against his chest, listening to his heart as it pounded against her ear and thundered against her palms.

He was shaking.

"You okay?" he whispered, his lips brushing her forehead.

She nodded, her voice nowhere to be found, driven away by the feel of his arms around her and how tightly he was holding her, as if he had been on the verge of losing something precious to him.

Gods, how she wanted to believe that.

It was all make believe though, a fantasy created by her mind as it interpreted how he had reacted and how he held her.

Wasn't it?

He pulled away before she could answer that question, casually rubbing the back of his neck. Water dripped from his silver-white hair and rolled down his cheeks, cascading past bright eyes of purest silver. They caught and held her, stirring her feelings back to the surface, the intensity of them making her deeply aware of him—his strength, his power, his dark allure.

She was as lost in him as she had been a decade ago, snared by the spell he cast by focusing with such intensity on her, making her feel as if she was the only other person in his universe.

"Didn't have problems like that back in London." He smiled but she saw straight through it.

The tiger had shaken him.

She wouldn't mention it. She would pretend she hadn't seen it. He was being strong and so was she, because all she really wanted to do was hold him and reassure herself that he was fine.

He was safe.

His smile faltered, turned strained, and he muttered to himself as he crossed the short span of earth to his backpack and clothes.

He grabbed his t-shirt from inside his fleece and she stared at his chest, at the scars that slashed across them. The sight of them transported her back five years again, to that night when she had felt she had been on the verge of dying. Seeing him fight Stellan that night had almost killed her.

"What's wrong?" Cavanaugh lowered the t-shirt to his side and approached her, every inch of him tensed and alert, and concern warming his grey eyes. "Is it the tiger?"

She shook her head and let the words tumble from her lips. "I was so frightened when you fought."

Without thinking, she stroked her fingers across his chest, following the marks that marred his pale skin. They had been so deep at the time, a wound that had forced him to shift back into his human form. They had bled badly, crimson pumping from the three slashes, spilling down his bare stomach and painting the snow. Her hand shook against him, hot tears rising even though she tried to hold them back.

The air thickened and he breathed hard, his intense gaze heating her inside, making her burn at a thousand degrees and ache to lift her eyes to his. She wanted to see that hunger in his eyes again, the heat that she had seen in them before.

The desire.

"Eloise," he husked, his voice scraping over gravel, stoking her need for him to a startling level, one that had her on the verge of surrendering to it.

Gods, she wanted to surrender to it.

She couldn't put herself through that much pain again though.

She pulled herself together, snatched her hand back and lowered her head. "I'm sorry."

"Fuck this shit." He shoved away from her, swiped his clothes from on top of his backpack and bundled them up in his arms as he strode away from her.

Eloise could only stare at him as he threw his clothes down on the ground around twenty metres from her, on the other side of the camp. He shoved his wet trunks down his legs, leaving him completely bare, and then tugged his dark grey trousers on. Anger laced his scent, born of frustration rather than the adrenaline rush of facing the tiger. He was angry with her. He seemed to be taking it out on his clothes too. She was surprised his boots didn't split apart at the seams as he pulled them open with force before shoving his feet into them.

She didn't understand him.

Since the day he had become the pride alpha ten years ago, he hadn't looked at her once, and he had been gone for five years. He had walked out of her life without as much as a backwards glance. He had made it clear that she had meant nothing to him and what had happened between them had been little more than hormones at play, a need he hadn't been able to deny.

But since she had walked into the nightclub, he hadn't taken his eyes off her, and the way he kept acting around her was taking her back beyond those ten years, to a point when they had been closer.

To a time when they had been together.

When the world hadn't been a dark place, because he had filled it with light.

He paused and looked across the narrow stretch of land that divided them, his grey eyes dark with the hunger she had wanted to see in them again for what felt like forever, the heat that she feared because it awakened something within her too.

Need.

Desire.

Hunger that consumed her.

It was still a three day trek to the village if the weather stayed as it was.

Gods help her but she wasn't sure she would make it.

No.

She was sure.

She wouldn't make it.

She was a moth drawn to his flame and it was only a matter of time before he set her on fire and had her burning so hot that it reduced her control to ashes.

CHAPTER 6

Cavanaugh followed Eloise through the thinning trees, his senses stretching around him, every scent and sight making him want to shift and explore in his snow leopard form. They had left camp at first light, after what had been one hell of an uncomfortable night for him.

Sharing the small tent with Eloise had been torture.

She had been right there beside him, shielded by a damned orange all-weather sleeping bag, but within his reach. He had breathed her in all night, and hadn't been able to sleep, and not only because of her presence just inches from him and the constant replays of when she had touched his chest that had filled his mind, making him ache for her.

He had been on high alert all night, his ears twitching with every noise outside the tent, no matter how harmless it had been. The snow leopard within him, the primal part of him, had demanded he stay awake and watch over Eloise, ready to protect her from any predators who might stray too close to his sleeping mate.

He had watched her slumber fitfully, wondering what haunted her dreams and whether it had anything to do with the scars on her wrists.

After mulling over everything that she had told him about Stellan and the pride over their dinner of protein bars, and analysing her behaviour where her wrists were concerned and how she didn't want him to see them, he had come to a dreadful conclusion.

She had been tied up more than once by the male he had left in charge of his kin.

She had gained the scars in her home village, not while she had been travelling and looking for him. He would kill Stellan for that cruel act alone. No one laid a hand on his Eloise without paying for it with their life.

Despite her bad dreams, she seemed brighter today. The colour was back on her cheeks and the dark circles beneath her eyes had finally disappeared, leaving her looking as beautiful as he had remembered.

As beautiful as the photograph of her that he cherished.

The cool mist of morning formed tiny crystal beads of water on her dark hair, causing the strands of her twisted knot at the back of her head to become spikes. It clung to the shoulders of her stone fleece too. The drops clinging to her transported him back to the countless times they had trekked out from the village through the snow in their leopard forms and how the white powder would cling to her beautiful silver coat. She had always stopped in the snow to shake it off, ending up with even more on her rather than less.

The last time that it had happened was as clear as day to him, a memory that would stay with him forever.

He had approached her and had licked the snow from her coat, and she had turned towards him and rubbed her cheek across his, the action tender and one that had touched him deeply. She had marked him with her scent, and had marked herself with his at the same time.

"Cavanaugh?" Her voice yanked him back to the forest and he stared through the trees at her for a second before realising that he had stopped walking and she was much further ahead of him, standing at the top of a steep dirt incline.

He shook his head and strode through the trees, stepping over the thick roots that littered the forest floor, and avoiding crushing the huge insects and small mammals under his boots. He wrapped his hands around the straps of his heavy backpack and adjusted it before scaling the incline, using the trees to navigate a path up to her, bracing his boots against their bases.

When he reached her, she was still frowning at him, her honey-coloured eyes warmed by concern.

"I didn't sleep much." It was the only explanation he was going to offer her. If she pushed, he might lie and say it was solely because he had wanted to protect her.

In reality, it was partly because he had been as hard as a steel pole in his trunks all night, aroused by the thought that she slept in only a flimsy top and shorts beneath her thick sleeping bag and the memories of her hands on his chest and the fire that had burned in her eyes.

Need he had felt in her and had commanded him to satisfy his mate.

She walked on ahead of him again, her hips swaying in her beige trousers, drawing his gaze down to her backside.

Cavanaugh scrubbed a hand over his mouth and groaned under his breath. He wasn't sure he could last another night sleeping close to her. He had never slept with her before, not even in such an innocent fashion, with them tucked into separate sleeping bags. If he couldn't find a spot to sleep in where he could have more distance between them, he was liable to leap on her and act on his desire. He wasn't sure that was a good idea, even though his body and his mind were screaming that it was.

It had been ten years since he had touched a woman, and since one had touched him. Ten years since he had been with Eloise. She had him fired up and constantly on edge around her, driven mad by his need of her. He had to rein it in though and somehow retain control, for both of their sakes.

He dragged his gaze away from her, forcing himself to take in the forest as he walked. They were moving away from the river, taking a shortcut to a point where they could cross it. From there, it was a steep and tricky trek up the side of the mountain. He checked his watch. It wasn't even noon. They were making good time. If they kept on like this, they might reach the top of the vertical ascent that lay ahead of them by nightfall.

Cavanaugh slowed down, not wanting that to happen. He had planned to stop at the base of the sheer climb up the side of one of the mountains— the only path to the village. Eloise wouldn't settle for that now. They would reach it by early afternoon. At best, he could convince her to stop halfway up the climb, where there was a cave his kin used as a shelter. It was large enough to provide them protection from any weather the mountain might throw at them, and for him to sleep a good distance from her.

Eloise looked back at him again, a frown marring her pretty face. Gods, she was beautiful, even when she was scowling at him and looked ready to box his ears for being slow. A touch of colour rose onto her cheeks and she hastily looked away, but not before he noticed the way her eyes had darkened.

Not with anger.

But with desire.

He groaned and picked up his pace, a slave to his need to be closer to her. She flicked another glance back at him as he neared her, a touch of nerves in her eyes now. She was breathtaking, flushed with life and vibrant, more like the woman he remembered her to be than the one she had become.

What had happened to her?

She had changed the day after the celebration of his ascension to the role of pride alpha, always avoiding him.

Had what they shared meant so little to her?

He hadn't been sure back then, part of him convinced that it had meant something but the rest of him arguing against it, but he had wanted to know. He still wanted to know. He had watched her whenever she had thought he wasn't looking, studying her for as long as he could without rousing suspicion, and he had sworn there had been hurt in her eyes at times.

He had convinced himself that he had only seen what he had wanted to see, because he had been hurting.

But things were different now.

She was different.

And it led him to believe that what they had shared had been real and they had both been hurt by his ascension.

They both felt something for the other.

Was it too late to make her see that?

A few days ago, he might have answered that question with a yes and resolved to make her change her mind. Since the events of yesterday, his mind and his heart said no. It wasn't too late for them.

He had been petrified when he had been swimming, on the verge of trying again to convince her to come into the water, and he had spotted the tiger stalking her. She had been completely unaware of it, her eyes locked on him and a hint of desire rolling off her.

His heart had stopped beating and had then exploded in his chest, the rush of it driving him into action. Everything primal within him, every instinct and sense, every feeling he owned, had demanded he protect her and take down the tiger if he had to go that far.

When the beast had finally backed off, he hadn't been able to stop himself from holding her. Then, she had touched him, telling him how scared she had been the night he had fought Stellan, making him believe that she had felt something for him and might still feel it. He had thought maybe he would get his wish.

She would be his again.

But she had pulled away.

Why?

Because of his status?

He hated it. He hated the wall it had built between them and he was determined to tear it down. He wouldn't allow anything to stand between them. He had been patient. He had waited for five long years, filled with a need to see her, to hear her voice and smell her scent again and feel her soft curves beneath his fingers. She had walked back into his life. She had come for him. He couldn't stop himself from reading into that and seeing it as a sign. His patience would pay off. He could heal the breach between them and win her back.

His wish would come true.

She would become his mate.

She led the way over the river and he followed her without really looking where he was going, wading through the water rather than traversing the rocks as she did, lost in his thoughts. When he reached the other bank and pulled himself up, she was looking at him again. Not with desire. This time she looked as if she was wondering whether he had lost his mind.

He hadn't lost that part of him.

He had lost his heart though.

It had been torn from his chest ten years ago and now he was slowly piecing it back together, gluing it with the hope that he could break down her defences and win her. He wanted her to surrender to him and their attraction to each other as she had a decade ago, showing him that she felt about him as he did about her, but part of him feared that if it happened before the full moon had risen, that it would only happen because he was her alpha.

It was the same fear that had always held him back.

The same rule that Stellan intended to use to make all the unmated females, regardless of their status, submit to him.

Cavanaugh didn't want such a union with her. It wasn't right.

It wasn't what he wanted for them.

He didn't want a mistress.

He wanted her to be his mate.

He wanted her to love him. To have that, he had to wait until he was free of his status. Only then would he be sure that what she felt for him was real.

It was getting more difficult by the second though. The longer he was around her, her scent filling his lungs and her curves tempting his eyes, the stronger his need to kiss her became. Every tree they passed, he fantasised about pinning her to it and stealing her breath with a kiss that would have her melting into him and moaning his name as she had the last night they had made love.

He palmed the growing bulge in his dark grey trousers, shifting it into a more comfortable position.

She glanced back at him again and he pretended he was fiddling with the hem of his charcoal fleece. He tugged it down a little so she wouldn't notice the effect she was having on him and kept walking, not daring to look at her until he felt her gaze leave him.

He sighed and pinched the bridge of his nose. He wasn't sure that even a vast distance between them would stop him from giving in to the pressing need to touch her, to kiss her and show her that he wanted her more than anything. He wasn't sure he would be able to last another night with her.

The need that had been gradually building inside him from the second he had spotted her in Underworld was reaching boiling point and he was burning for her.

The forest began to thin as they ascended and the ground turned rocky underfoot. Eloise continued to lead, stealing more of his focus away from the world around him as they followed a steep trail up the mountainside. There were less predators for him to worry about up here. Tigers continued until several thousand metres up into the mountains, where their territories clashed with those of the snow leopards, but leopards were scarce up here and clouded leopards remained in the forest below.

Eloise skidded back a step on the loose stony ground and huffed as she regained her footing, muttering beneath her breath. Cavanaugh guessed she was blaming the boots he had bought for her again. They were probably too new for such a trek, their thick soles and deep unworn grips making them slippery over some terrains, but they were far better than the ones she had sported before. He doubted she would have made it this far without falling flat on her face, or worse, if he had left her to attempt to traverse the forest and the mountain in her worn out boots.

She trudged on ahead and he closed the distance between them as the path widened, trailing through the odd patch of scrub on the desolate mountainside. It was grey as far as the eye could see. Only the occasional group of trees that were hardy enough to survive at such an elevation broke up the monotonous landscape on the slope stretching ahead of him. The path was a paler wiggly line slowly ascending towards one such patch of trees. Beyond those, the mountain suddenly rose up as a vertical wall that would challenge the most adept of human climbers.

In the distance behind him, a call went out, a low mournful sound that had his ears pricking. A snow leopard. He felt the big cat's need beating within him too. It was a male looking for a receptive female.

It wanted a mate.

Eloise looked back at him, the sprinkling of rose across her cheeks saying she had heard the call too and knew what it meant. Cavanaugh prowled towards her, narrowing his eyes on hers with each step closer he came to her, and she dropped her gaze, the colour on her cheeks darkening.

Gods, he wanted to kiss her when she looked so shy and beautiful.

"We should hurry if we're going to start our ascent today." She scurried away from him and he grunted, wanted to growl out his frustration over the way she kept escaping him, and then stalked after her, driven by a need to hunt her.

His snow leopard form shifted restlessly beneath his skin, wanting out. He wanted to transform and obey his compelling need to walk for a while in his other form, but he couldn't. It was safer for both of them if he remained in his human one. The big cats in the area would view him more as a threat in this form. In his other form, they might want to fight over territory with him.

He didn't want to fight in front of Eloise, not after her soft confession last night.

He didn't want her to be afraid for him again.

She scrambled up the steepest part of the path to join the one that intersected it and led along the ridge towards the trees and the vertical wall of rock they needed to scale.

Cavanaugh followed her, only briefly looking behind him towards the direction the call had come from, unable to deny his desire to see the snow leopard. He hadn't seen one in years, except for himself in the mirror of the playroom. He hated seeing himself in his snow leopard form though, because it made him think of Eloise. It took him back to all the times they had trekked together and played in their cat forms, and he ended up aching with a need to see her that lasted for days.

She stopped at the base of the wall in amidst the trees and looked up the height of it. Several hundred metres of sheer grey rock, with few handholds and only one place to rest. It was a challenge he relished. This was the point he had always looked forwards to when journeying to or from the village.

Just the sight of it had his heart beating harder, pumping adrenaline through his veins as his body prepared for the exhilaration and strain of the ascent.

He slipped his pack off and undid it, taking out everything that was necessary, including a smaller pack that would have to suffice from this point forwards. It was large enough to accommodate his sleeping bag, the food, the canteen, and a change of clothes. He stashed the bigger pack in a crevice where no one would find it.

Eloise was already stripping down to her base layer of a long-sleeved thermal top. He stared at her, unabashed even when she glanced his way. He couldn't take his eyes off her. The tight top hugged her breasts and stirred hunger within him, reawakening the fierce need to draw her into his arms and kiss her.

Cavanaugh dragged his eyes away from her and busied himself by following her lead, removing his fleece and t-shirt, and replacing them with a similar black thermal top. It was chilly with only the thin layer, but snow leopards could cope with extreme cold, and it wouldn't be long before the exertion of scaling the sheer rock face had him warmed up. Even in such a flimsy layer, he would end up hot and sweaty by the time they reached the small cave halfway up the several hundred metres high sheer wall.

He stepped into his harness and made sure it was tight and secure around his hips before picking up the one for Eloise.

She tensed as he approached her, triggering his desire to stalk her, to hunt her and make her surrender to him. He tamped down that need and swallowed hard, fighting to get his mind off what he was about to do and shut down the way his body was reacting to just the thought of it.

It was no use.

The moment he kneeled in front of her, his gaze level with her hips, he lost the battle against his body. All of his blood rushed south, making him instantly hard in his trousers. He drew in a deep breath and it only made things worse, filling his senses with her scent. He wet his lips and held the black harness out to her. She stepped into it, caught her left boot on the straps, and jerked forwards. Her hands came down on his shoulders to steady her, sending fire blazing along his bones.

He growled and she snatched them back, a little gasp escaping her.

He hadn't meant it as a threat and she knew it. She had sensed the desire within him, the need that pounded in his blood, and had heard it in his hungry growl.

"Sorry," she whispered and he mentally cursed her for apologising again.

She could touch all she wanted, as long as she initiated things. That was the rule he had to keep in place so he would know that she wanted him, that whatever happened between them wasn't because he was her alpha.

He had drawn a line between them and she had to be the one to cross it.

She had to be the one to show him that what they had shared a decade ago hadn't been one-sided. She had been in love with him.

As he was in love with her.

He tugged the harness up her legs, fastened it in place around her hips, and stepped away from her, giving himself a moment to bring his hungers back under control. He grabbed the rope they would be using for the ascent and tugged it, testing its strength. He threaded the rope through his harness and made sure it was secure before taking a final deep breath.

Cavanaugh turned around to face her.

She stood a short distance away, retying her rich brown hair, preparing herself for the climb. It needed zero distractions and one hundred percent of their focus. There were no points on the climb where they could attach themselves to anchors in the rocks. Protecting the pride meant leaving nothing on the wall that could be used by humans to reach the top and the hidden valley there.

The only security he and Eloise would have was each other.

He closed the gap between them and threaded the rope through her harness, his gaze fixed on his work. It was nice to finally be linked to her in a way, even if it was only through a rope. He tugged it, checking it was secure and wouldn't slip free of the harness. He needed to know that it would take her weight if she slipped.

He couldn't lose her.

He had spent too long without her as it was.

He would sooner die than face the rest of his life without her.

He lifted his gaze to her face, immediately losing himself in her deep honey-coloured eyes. They bravely held his, even when her heart accelerated in his ears, quickening her breathing with it, and the sharp scent of nerves laced her sweet scent.

"Cavanaugh?" she whispered breathlessly, her soft voice teasing him into drawing her closer to him, tugging on the rope that connected them and not stopping until she was mere inches from him.

Her head tilted back, her eyes still holding his.

His heart beat harder and he couldn't breathe as he stared down into her eyes, the air growing thick around them once more.

He wanted to kiss her, needed just one kiss to build his confidence, not just for the climb ahead of them but for his battle to win her, but he wasn't sure how she would react to it.

His fingers flexed around the smooth rope.

He backed off a step and let it slip through his grasp, and turned away from her, lifting his head towards the sheer rock wall.

He couldn't kiss her, and not only because he had vowed she would be the one to make the first move.

He stared at the dark grey cliff face that loomed over him.

He couldn't kiss her because he didn't need to try to climb it with a painful rejection clouding his mind.

One second was all it would take.

One second in which his focus slipped.

One second that would spell the end of their forever.

CHAPTER 7

Eloise gripped with her left hand and swung herself across to her right, reaching for the next hold she had spotted there. She caught it with the tips of her fingers and pulled herself forwards, improving her grip on the narrow gap in the grey rock wall.

She felt Cavanaugh's gaze on her again, hot and piercing, sending a rush of heat through her. He had to stop looking at her that way.

Her concentration was already shot. She couldn't stop thinking about how Cavanaugh had reacted when she had touched him at the base of the cliff, using her hands on his shoulders to steady herself. Hunger had flashed in his eyes and his low growl had sent a hot shiver bolting through her, filling her with a potent need to skim her hands over his broad shoulders and tempt him into kissing her.

She had thought that he would when he had pulled her towards him, his eyes filled with desire that she could scent on him. He had released her but she knew he had come close to kissing her, had somehow mastered his desire and stopped himself. Why? She had cursed him for not going through with it. He had fired her up and then backed away, leaving her head filled with thoughts of what might have been and questions about why he would kiss her, why he had stopped, and what the hell was wrong with her. She shouldn't want him to kiss her. She had to fight her attraction to him. It was for the best.

Her heart called her a liar.

It wasn't for the best. Resisting him and her need of him was driving her crazy.

He had been on her mind all day, stealing her focus away from the world around her during their trek. She hadn't been able to stop thinking about him since he had woken her this morning before dawn, rousing her from a wicked dream of him. She had opened her eyes to find him lying beside her, propped up on his elbow, his face above hers. His silver-white hair had been mussed, as if he had been tugging it all night, ploughing his fingers through it. It had tempted her to do the same. His grey eyes had been warm and bright, filled with a strange light that had left her feeling he was happy and it was because she was with him.

She pushed it all out of her mind and tried to focus on the climb.

Cavanaugh looked back down at her again, sending another fierce hot shiver through her. He really had to stop looking at her like that.

She couldn't concentrate whenever he did and found herself watching him as he climbed instead.

He was an expert climber, far more agile than any of the other males in their pride. She had forgotten just how skilled and powerful he was. He made climbing the sheer wall of the mountain look easy, the thick muscles of his arms working hard beneath his tight black thermal top.

Cavanaugh looked down and paused with only his right hand and the tip of his left boot on a hold. Her stomach turned. She trusted him, but she wished he would hold on with both hands and feet. If he fell, she wasn't sure she could support his weight. She would try, but deep in her heart she knew that the force of the rope that linked them snapping taut would pry her away from the rocks and have her falling with him. They were already close to one hundred metres above the path. If they fell from where they were now, they would definitely break enough bones to leave them vulnerable to the predators that made the mountains their homes.

He swung back towards the wall and reached for another hold, kicking off on his left foot to propel himself upwards. He snagged the small section of rock jutting from the cliff face and pulled himself up, finding another hold for his right hand and then for his feet. She couldn't move as he did. She didn't have the courage or the faith in her abilities.

He looked back down again and she silently thanked him for keeping all hands and feet on their holds this time, and for checking on her. She had climbed with many from her pride, but none had ever checked on her as he did, watching her with concern in his striking dark grey eyes.

He smiled before shoving off with his left foot and leaping an insane distance off to his right, catching a hold that seemed invisible to her. Her heart rocketed and she came close to shouting at him, but the grin on his face when he looked back down at her had her falling silent and smiling back at him.

How long had it been since he had climbed like this? He was loving every second of it, thriving on the thrill of it all as they slowly ascended. She had forgotten just how deeply his love of danger and adventure ran in his blood. He lived for challenges like this.

She had missed this male, the one who was carefree and filled with life, energetic and excited.

Between the times when she had been thinking dangerous thoughts about Cavanaugh, she had thought about how much he had changed during his time as the pride's alpha. Seeing him relishing the climb only made those changes clearer to her. She had missed how much his position had weighed on him and how hard it had been for him, but she hadn't failed to notice how cold and distant he had grown over the years as their alpha, always lost deep in thought.

She could see now that a part of him had died and now it had been revived. He had found it again.

And she was making him return to the pride.

Eloise wanted to call out to him and tell him to turn around, to come back down and forget everything she had told him about the pride. She wanted to make him leave this place before it was too late for him and she was forced to watch this light inside him die again.

She didn't think she could bear seeing it happen and knowing she was responsible for it this time.

She didn't want him to lose his smile again.

"Cavanaugh," she started and he looked down at her again, pausing around five metres above her, the rope hanging slack between them. She found another hold and pulled herself up, making sure she was safe before she opened her mouth to speak.

"Remember how we used to climb like this?" He grinned at her, his grey eyes bright and entrancing her, taking her back several decades to the times he was asking her to recall.

She nodded. "You were always trying to show off."

She bit her tongue when he frowned, afraid she had overstepped the mark. For a moment, a split-second, she had forgotten that he was her pride's alpha. He had been that male from decades ago, the one he had asked her to remember.

The one who had stolen her heart.

He barked out a laugh. "I wanted to impress you."

She almost lost her hold on the rocks when she jerked her head up to meet his eyes. They were sincere, filled with honesty and something else she feared naming. Warmth. Tenderness. Maybe even love.

She pushed past the sadness that threatened to well up inside her, the fear that this was all a fantasy, and managed a smile. "You impressed me the time you fell almost seventy metres into the snow below. I told you not to be a crazy son of a bitch but would you listen? You almost gave me a heart attack!"

She had thought she had lost him, just as she had feared she had the night he had fled into the darkness after his fight against Stellan, bleeding from a terrible wound.

His frown faded, his expression softening dangerously, turning him even more handsome and making her heart race. She wanted to look away but forced herself to hold his gaze, to see the man she had lost all those years ago. He was here with her now.

She cursed the tears that wanted to rise into her eyes as he smiled and shrugged.

"I was a stupid bastard. I should have listened to you. You always were right." He lowered his gaze away from her and frowned again. "I'm sorry I made you have kittens… but think of it as payback for all the times you scared me half to death."

The corners of his sensual lips tugged back into a half smile.

She glared at him. "What are you trying to say?"

His smile grew. "That I saved your backside more times than I can count."

Eloise huffed and refused to acknowledge that, even though it was true. He had saved her life countless times, but then he had always been the one who had been pushing her to take risks and court danger. She had wanted to stay at his side, had been afraid he would race ahead of her and leave her behind, or he would find another partner for his adventures, so she had pushed herself hard, struggling to keep up with him.

She spied another hold just a metre above her left hand and focused on it as she kicked off, launching herself up to it. She snagged it, dug her claws in and hauled herself up, scrabbling around for another hold for her right hand. She found a crevice and slipped her fingers into it, and then secured her feet, breathing hard. Maybe she was still pushing herself too hard in an effort to stay at his side.

"You good?" Cavanaugh said with a laugh in his voice. "Because I'd hate to have to come down there and save your arse."

"Gods, you're so funny," she muttered and flicked a glance up at him.

His smile stole her breath, and it was all because of her. It was because she was talking to him, not as her alpha but as she had so long ago, back when they had been friends. More than friends.

She stared up at him, every inch of her heating through as his grey eyes twinkled at her and the wind tousled the soft spikes of his silver-white hair. Gods, he was gorgeous.

Guilt flooded her again and she had to look away to stop herself from telling him to turn around and go back. The pride needed him. She couldn't let them down.

Eloise looked around for another hold. There was one, but it was further than the last, a stretch for her. No, she could make it. She had good holds for her feet, firm enough to give her the leverage she needed to make it that far.

"I saved your arse a few times too." She stretched with her right arm and kicked off with her right foot.

The rock beneath it crumbled.

Eloise shrieked as she dropped.

Cavanaugh grunted and grabbed the rope that connected them with his left hand and dug in with his right, his fear flashing across his face and beating through her blood.

"Eloise!" He gritted his teeth and strained as she fell, her hands scrabbling over the rocks, seeking a hold.

There was none.

The rope snapped tight between them.

Cavanaugh grunted again but maintained his position.

Eloise slammed into the cliff face.

Her head smacked off a protruding rock.

Pain blazed across her left temple and arm.

Cavanaugh roared her name.

The world went dark.

CHAPTER 8

Cavanaugh's heart pounded so hard he felt dizzy. He shook his head and forced himself to focus on Eloise. She dangled from the end of the rope, spinning slowly around thirty feet below him, bent in the middle with her arms and legs dangling beneath her.

"Eloise, Baby, come on," he whispered, staring down at her and fighting to get his fear under control and subdue his panic so his damned senses would focus and he could stop thinking the worst.

She wasn't dead.

She couldn't be.

He closed his eyes and drew in a deep breath, the muscles of his right arm screaming in protest as he supported both his weight and hers. It didn't matter if he tore his muscles. All that mattered was Eloise.

He focused on his breathing, until his panic began to subside and the rush of his blood and tremulous beat of his heart in his ears faded and he could begin to distinguish the sounds of the world around him again.

Birds called down in the valley. Wind stirred the treetops.

Eloise's heartbeat sounded in his ears.

She was unconscious.

He breathed a sigh and gritted his teeth as he strained with his left arm, hauling the rope clutched in his fist up to his shoulder, dragging her dead weight upwards. His fangs extended and he placed the rope between his lips and bit down, digging his teeth in but careful not to damage the rope. It needed to last until the shelter at least. He had another rope in his pack that he could use to get them up the second half of the climb once Eloise had recovered.

Cavanaugh drew in a deep breath to steady his nerves. He was quick enough. He was strong enough. He could do this. He just needed enough slack in the rope to wrap it around him and let his body take the weight of Eloise as he hauled her up to him.

He crushed the panic as it slowly began to rise again, obliterating it, and let go of the rope. His fangs ached, bearing Eloise's weight in the split-second it took for him to reach and snag the rope further down.

He gripped the rope with his left hand, released it from his teeth and repeated the process, pulling Eloise up towards him, clenching the rope in his fangs, and then letting go of the rope to quickly grab hold of it again. He wrapped the rope around him, over his right shoulder and under his left arm, careful not to slam Eloise into the cliff as he worked. Once the slack was around him, he began hauling her up with his left hand, wrapping the rope around himself as he went.

When she was level with him, he looped the last of the rope around him so she dangled beside him.

He released the rope and caught hold of her harness instead. He hoped to the gods she stayed unconscious for this next part, because it was going to be hair-raising at best. He fumbled with the carabineers on the back of her harness and then jostled her so she ended up behind him, her back to his. He clipped her securely to his harness, unwound the rope from around his torso, and then wrapped it around both of them, so it looped over one shoulder and under the opposite arm, tightly binding them together with their packs wedged between them.

The fingers of his right hand ached from holding both of their weight and he grabbed the nearest hold with his left, alleviating the pressure on his right arm. He paused for a moment and scouted the path ahead, already struggling to bear the extra weight.

One hundred metres above him to the right there was a ledge. The shelter. He could make it. He had to make it.

Cavanaugh grabbed the first hold and pulled himself up, carefully so as not to swing Eloise. He needed her weight to remain right behind him, in line with his own. He gritted his teeth and grunted as he reached for the next hold, caught it and hauled them up higher. He dug his toes into a narrow gap in the rock and pushed up, stretching for the next hold.

It was hard going with her added weight. Sweat trickled down his spine as he forced himself to keep moving, his arms aching and fingers sore. Blood spotted them, the rocks tearing their tips to shreds. He kept going, grunting with each new handhold he found and each short distance he traversed, closing the gap between him and the shelter.

He tested the next hold and growled as it gave way, crumbling and dropping down the rock face. He veered right instead, heading for a long vertical gash in the grey rock that he had used on previous climbs.

Cavanaugh looked up at the ledge. Fifty metres. He could rest once he was there and then take care of Eloise. He hadn't managed to get a look at her injuries. He wasn't sure how bad they were.

He scaled another five metres using the gash in the rock. It was just wide enough for him to fit both hands inside it, and uneven enough that he had some good holds. The bones in his hands burned. The muscles in his arms and shoulders ached. He couldn't stop though. Not yet. Not until the shelter.

He needed to get Eloise to the shelter.

He needed to get her to safety.

He forced himself to continue, pushing beyond the limits of his body, unwilling to give up.

"Cav…" The soft murmur of his name made him pause and he looked over his left shoulder at Eloise. Was she conscious?

He wasn't sure. He felt certain that if she had been aware of her predicament, she would have been panicking.

"I'm here, Eloise." He gripped the rocks with his right hand and reached around with his left, touching her hip. "I've got you, Baby."

She murmured something and her weight increased, pulling him backwards. He grabbed the rock face with both hands to secure himself and sighed. She had been conscious, but she must have been keeping her eyes closed, and had only remained awake for as long as it had taken for her to hear that she was going to be alright.

He would never let anything happen to her.

He redoubled his effort, every shred of his strength and focus fixed on reaching the ledge and getting her to safety. Each metre closer he came to the shelter, the climb became harder, and he had to keep pushing himself, using his memories of Eloise and his love for her to give him the strength to keep climbing.

When he reached the ledge, he hauled himself onto it and crawled to the narrow low mouth of the cave before collapsing on his side. He breathed hard, staring into the darkness of the cave, every inch of him shaking from the exertion and from the fear that now swept through him, tearing him apart inside.

He might have lost her.

He hadn't allowed himself to feel any fear when he had been climbing, but he couldn't stop it from bombarding him now. He reached behind him and clutched her waist, feeling her flesh give beneath his fingers and listening to her slow but steady breathing. She was safe.

But freezing cold.

It drove him into action, pushing the fear out of his mind again and the fatigue from his body. He unwrapped the rope from around them, managed to get her unclipped from his harness, and rolled over to face her. She lay on her side, her head resting on the rock. A small pool of blood had already formed beneath it, dripping from her temple.

Cavanaugh eased onto his knees and carefully manoeuvred her onto her back. She didn't wince or moan. She remained still and silent. He didn't like it. He wanted her to say his name again. He needed to know that she was going to be alright. He touched the deep cut on her left temple and the one in her dark hair near it. There was a tear in the left arm of her thermal long-sleeve top too, revealing a gash beneath it and black bruising. He tried to be gentle as he checked her arm, pressing in to feel the bone and see whether she had broken it.

Just bruised.

He breathed a sigh of relief and swept his fingers through her hair, squinting as he used the fading light to check the cut there and the one on her temple. They were already healing. In a day or two, they would be gone.

Cavanaugh shuffled backwards into the cave, squeezing through the tight entrance, and caught her under her arms and pulled her with him, dragging her inside. The cave opened up beyond the entrance, enough that he could stand hunched over. He lifted the top half of her off the ground and pulled her along as he backed towards the end of the cave where it was warmer. She moaned as her left foot bumped over a rock.

"Sorry," he muttered and carefully laid her down.

He took his pack off, unrolled his sleeping bag, and pulled her onto it to get her off the cold hard ground. He used his heightened vision to find the small solar-powered light he had in the backpack and turned it on. Blue-white light chased the shadows back. He couldn't light a fire. The smoke would accumulate in the cave. He needed to get her warm though, and there was only one way it was going to happen.

His body got the wrong idea, his cock stiffening in his trousers.

He resisted palming it and set about his work, hoping his erection would go away if he focused on looking after Eloise. He took the pack off her shoulders, stripped off her harness and her cold damp clothes and her boots, leaving her in only her underwear, and then grabbed her orange sleeping bag and unzipped it. He laid it over her while he stripped off, kicking his boots across the cave and tossing his harness. He spread his thermal top and trousers over his pack so they would dry. His underwear joined them.

Cavanaugh looked down at her. If she woke to find him naked, she wasn't going to be very happy with him, but he didn't have a choice. She needed warmth and he could give that to her. The quicker he could get her warm, the sooner she would recover.

He rolled her over, so she was on her own sleeping bag, and unzipped his blue one. He settled her on top of it, laid down beside her and zipped the two sleeping bags together, making one big one. Once he had finished his task, he closed his eyes and focused.

He ground his teeth and growled through his fangs as he began the transformation, his bones snapping out of place and reshaping, forming a new skeleton beneath his burning flesh. He snarled as quietly as he could to avoid disturbing her as a thick long tail sprouted from the base of his spine, and his feet and hands widened, his fingers and toes changing into soft claw-tipped pads. His face shifted, his jaw snapping out of place and growing wider as his cheeks puffed up and his nose flattened. His ears rang as they increased in sensitivity and moved upwards, becoming rounded as they settled on top of his head. Silver fur spotted with darker rosettes rippled over his body, thick and lush, designed to trap heat and keep him warm.

Cavanaugh huffed as his transformation finished and shuffled closer to Eloise beneath the thick layer of the sleeping bags. He wrapped his body around her as much as he could, ensuring his fur would warm her, and curled his tail around her right leg.

He licked the wound on her head, cleaning the blood away, and then the one on her arm. His saliva would help the cuts heal too, quickening the whole process. When he had finished, he looked down at her, every male instinct he possessed telling him that she was his mate, even though she didn't know it.

Yet.

He fought the urge that welled up inside him but it was too strong and he gave in to it, rubbing his cheek against hers and then against her breasts, marking her with his scent. He wanted her to smell like him.

He needed it.

More than anything.

He closed his eyes and savoured being so close to her, tucked against her side, feeling her breathing and her heart beating. She would be upset with him if she woke to find him holding her, and possibly embarrassed too, but he didn't care. He wouldn't let her go. She felt too good pressed against him like this.

It felt right.

It felt as if he had found a vital piece of himself that had been lost for ten years, a piece that completed the shattered part of him and made it whole again. That part was his heart. Eloise had put it back together for him and it felt stronger than before.

It rested in her hands and it always had. His mate had held it for decades without ever knowing it. His Eloise. He couldn't hold back the truth any longer.

When she woke, he would find a way to tell her.

It was time she knew why he had gone away.

It was time she knew that she was his fated mate.

CHAPTER 9

Eloise moaned and frowned. Her head throbbed, feeling as if someone had grabbed hold of it and shaken it so hard that her brain was still rattling around and banging against her skull. She winced and tried to open her eyes. Bright blue-white light assaulted them and she flinched away from it, jerking backwards.

Into something solid and warm, and very male.

Her eyes shot open and she went rigid as she realised that she was on Cavanaugh's lap, in the cradle between his thighs as he sat cross-legged, his arms wrapped around her, holding her to his chest.

Cavanaugh's naked chest.

Cavanaugh's very naked lap.

Her head shot up, an ache ricocheting across the back of her eyes in response, and she stilled. He wasn't smirking at her as she had expected. He was sound asleep, his head resting against the dark rock wall behind him and his sensual lips parted as he breathed slowly. She looked down at herself, mortified to discover that he wasn't the only one who was naked. She was only wearing her bra and knickers.

Eloise grabbed the sleeping bag that was wrapped around them both, trying to cover herself. The frantic action jerked Cavanaugh forwards. His chin dipped towards his chest, and he grunted as he frowned and slowly opened his eyes. Hers shot wide.

He smiled in exactly the mischievous way she had anticipated and did something that threatened to shatter her self-control.

He tightened his grip on her, hauling her closer to him, the muscles of his arms bulging as he wrapped them around her.

Heat scalded her cheeks.

His smile widened. "No need to be embarrassed. We've shared body heat before... and in far more interesting ways."

"That was a long time ago." Eloise pressed her hands to his chest and shoved, trying to break free of his grip.

He didn't let her go. He stared at her face and tipped his chin up in a short jerky motion. "Turn towards your right. I want to check your temple. You took a nasty knock. You had me worried."

Her heart warmed in her chest at the truth in those words as concern filled his grey eyes. She did as he wanted, turning her left cheek to him.

"It's nothing," she said, her voice failing her as his breath fanned across her cheek.

He was leaning closer.

She struggled to breathe normally as he brushed his lips across her temple, sending a hot shiver dancing through her, igniting the need she kept denying and elevating it to such a level that she wavered, on the brink of turning her face towards him. If she did, their lips would touch.

Would he kiss her?

Was that what she wanted?

Yes, and no. She wasn't sure what she wanted anymore. She wanted the old Cavanaugh back, she wanted the future she had foolishly dreamed they would have, but she couldn't have either of those things. She could never have them. He was her pride's alpha now.

"Eloise," he husked, his voice deeper than she had ever heard it, filled with the desire that she could scent on him and could feel pressed against her right hip.

"I was distracted," she said, trying to distract herself again and pretend that he wasn't aroused, and she wasn't either, because this wasn't what she wanted. She wanted him, but not like this. Not when it would mean nothing. "It was my fault."

"Distracted?" His voice hadn't risen above a wicked murmur that did funny things to her insides, heating them and making them flip and quiver. "I'm feeling distracted... gods, you feel good... better than I remembered."

She nodded and he groaned, and she cursed herself when she realised he thought she was nodding about feeling good in his arms. She had to get him thinking about something other than how close they were, and had to get herself to stop thinking about it at the same time. He felt too good against her, his hard body warming hers, his skin silken and tempting her into stroking her fingers over it.

She swallowed hard, got a grip on herself and forced the words out. "I was distracted."

He rubbed his nose across her temple, nudging her, his breath hot and moist, tempting her into kissing him. "Distracted by what?"

Her eyes slipped shut and she almost rubbed against him in return.

No.

Eloise found the strength to pull back from him, stopping him from rubbing and kissing her, teasing her into surrendering to him. It seemed that he was the only, constant source of distraction in her life.

"You." She looked away from him.

"Then it was my fault." He sounded normal again and she risked a glance at him, finding that he looked it too. He frowned at her and then sighed. "I should have known better than to talk while we were climbing... but I was enjoying it."

He had been enjoying it?

She had been enjoying it too. For a moment, she'd had the old Cavanaugh back, and it had been wonderful.

She stared into his eyes, wishing she were strong enough to ask him outright about what had happened between them and whether it had meant anything to him. She wasn't though, not right now. He still had her muddled, unsure whether she was coming or going, but fighting her feelings every step of the way. She couldn't give in to them, no matter how much she wanted to let everything go and have a moment of madness with him.

Her feelings for him had never died, but they had never been this strong either. He had awakened them in her again and somehow he had made them grow, pulling her deeper under his spell and forging a stronger connection between them.

He studied her face, his grey eyes sharp and focused.

She wasn't sure what to say to him. She wanted to say that she had been enjoying their easy banter too, but she couldn't get the words out. She couldn't lay her heart on the line again, not after what had happened and not when nothing could come of it.

She could only be a temporary thing to him, not his sole female. He could never reciprocate the feelings she harboured for him.

"How is your mother?"

Those four words leaving his lips chilled her to her marrow and instantly extinguished all of the heat he had built inside her.

She looked away from him, at her knees and his right arm. "She died six months after you left."

"Shit." He drew her closer to him and her resistance crumbled as his heat encased her, his scent filling her nostrils and comforting her. She leaned her head on his left shoulder and pressed her forehead against his neck, and stared beyond his arm, at the corner of the cave. He sighed and stroked her left arm, the soft motion giving her something to focus on other than the pain that had bubbled up inside her heart on having to tell him what had happened. "I'm sorry. I didn't know. I hate that I wasn't there for you, Eloise."

She did too.

She turned her face towards him and fought the memories of that day and the ones that had followed it, and how much she had longed for Cavanaugh to be there, holding her as he was now, giving her the comfort and strength she had needed.

He dropped his head and pressed his lips to her forehead.

"Gods, I'm sorry," he whispered against her skin and clutched her closer. "I bet she was mad at me for leaving."

Eloise smiled at the harsh self-reproach in his voice and nodded. "She was angry with you."

He sighed. "Something in your tone says she was more than angry with me, and about more than me leaving. She made it pretty clear whenever she looked at me that she hated me after I had to take the position of alpha."

She tried to shake her head but barely shifted it. It felt too heavy, as weighed down as her heart was right now.

He already knew the truth. There was little point in lying to him, even if saying it straight was disrespectful to him.

"She didn't hate you for taking the position... she hated you for leaving me."

He stilled right down to his breathing.

Eloise wasn't sure what to do. Part of her wanted to push out of his arms while he was distracted by what she had said, and the rest wanted to wrap her own arms around him and tell him she was sorry for dealing such a low blow. She didn't know what she was doing anymore. She didn't want to hurt him, but sometimes she couldn't stop herself from lashing out one way or another. Ten years of pent up hurt wanted to burst out of her and she couldn't hold it back.

"Eloise..." His voice dropped an octave and he tried to pull her closer but she resisted, finally finding the strength to push him away and gain some space between them. His silver eyebrows dipped low above his grey eyes as they searched hers, darting from one to the other. "You really think I wanted to take that position... that I wanted to leave you?"

Gods, she didn't know what to think when he said things like that. She wanted to believe him. She wanted to believe that he had been as in love with her as she had been with him, and that it had hurt him too, but she couldn't get past her own hurt.

She couldn't get past the pain of spending five years watching him with other women, and the next five alone and afraid, sure she would never see him again and would be the next to die at Stellan's hands.

She couldn't get past how he had never tried to talk with her or let her know the things he was telling her now.

"You do," he whispered, resignation and pain surfacing in his eyes. "You really do."

"There's nothing else for me to think." She shoved out of his arms, fell onto her knees and wrestled free of the blankets.

She shot to her feet, almost cracking her head on the low ceiling of the cave, and began to pace, hunched over and breathing hard, needing the space or she was going to explode. She wanted to turn on him and give him hell, just as she had wanted a million times before, but just like all those times, she reined in her anger and crushed it out of existence.

Because he was her pride's alpha.

She could hate him all she wanted for what had happened, but she still had to respect him.

"Eloise." He reached for her.

"Don't Eloise me," she snapped and paced away from him, towards the entrance of the cave where the air was chilly and fresh. She took deep breaths of it, using it to cool her head before she did something she would regret or said something she couldn't take back.

He lowered his hand onto the sleeping bag, over his knee, and heaved another sigh. "I left because of you."

Her lips parted. He had done what?

She scowled at him. "No... you left because Stellan defeated you and you wanted to get away from being the alpha of the pride... you left because you hated it at the village... you..."

"Left because I couldn't bear seeing you drifting away from me."

She shook her head, a chill skating down her spine, and folded her arms across her chest. She rubbed them, trying to stop herself from feeling cold to the bone. It wasn't possible. He couldn't have left because of her. He just couldn't. It was too much. How did he expect her to react to it? Why hadn't he sought her out and told her why he was leaving? She might have stopped him.

She might have gone with him.

She shook her head again, tears burning her eyes. It was too cruel to say these things to her now, after everything she had been through because of him.

"No... please, Cavanaugh... don't lie to me."

Because she couldn't bear it. It was tearing down her defences, even when it changed nothing. He utterly laid waste to what was left of her barriers when he rose onto his feet, the sleeping bags falling away to reveal his naked body.

Her mouth went dry. She tried to look away but her eyes were too occupied with drifting over every inch of him, reacquainting herself with just how lean and powerful he was, honed and god-like, the epitome of a strong male.

"Eloise," he husked, burning her resolve to ashes, "I left because I wanted you and I couldn't have you."

She barked out a short laugh at that, a bitter taste on her tongue as she glared at him. "You could have had me. You could have just ordered me into your bed."

His eyes darkened and she took a step back, a ripple of awareness travelling through her. She had pushed too far and too hard, and she had hurt him with her callous words. Her Cavanaugh would never do such a thing. She knew it in her heart. He would never use the rules of their pride to force her to sleep with him.

She had just put him on the same despicable level as Stellan.

"I'm sorry." She covered her mouth and shook her head, hating how feeble her apology sounded.

His jaw tensed and he looked away from her, his gaze downcast. "I see. So… you're bringing me back to the pride to trade one monster for another."

"No, Cavanaugh, that isn't what I—"

He silenced her with a glare, his eyes glowing silver around his wide pupils.

"Shouldn't you speak to me with a little more damned respect?" he barked and she took another step back. Her gaze darted to her feet, but not before she caught the regret that shone in his eyes. "I need some fucking air."

He swiped his trousers from the pile of clothing near their packs, pulled them on and strode towards her. She ducked to one side and pressed herself against the wall as he passed, and closed her eyes as he crawled through the entrance of the cave and disappeared from view.

Eloise slid down the wall and onto her backside. She drew her knees up to her chest and stared at the wall opposite, listening to Cavanaugh as he paced the ledge outside the shelter. She wanted to apologise and explain, but he radiated fury at a level she could sense and her instincts were screaming a warning at her. She heeded them, willing to give him a moment to cool off because she knew he wouldn't go anywhere without her.

He was angry with her, but he wouldn't leave her.

Her mind drifted over everything he had said. He hadn't wanted to be the pride alpha. He hadn't wanted to leave her.

But he had left her.

He had left her without a word. Without a goodbye. It had cemented her feeling that he hadn't cared about her, not in the way she cared about him. What if she had been wrong all these years?

She had thought about going after him when he had left, but it had been dark, a moonless night, and Stellan had been swift to warn everyone that he would kill anyone he caught attempting to leave. She had never been as afraid as she had been that night—both for her own life and for Cavanaugh's. Her mother had convinced her to wait until daybreak, and somehow she had managed it, only to find it snowing heavily. Even if she had managed to slip unnoticed from the village, she wouldn't have been able to track him with the fresh powder covering his trail.

Her mother had comforted her by saying that Cavanaugh would return and Eloise had believed her. She had realised too late that her mother had said whatever it had taken to keep her in the village and safe. Her mother had confessed it to her on her deathbed and Eloise had reassured her that she wasn't angry with her, even when part of her had been. The rest of her had been filled with a need to find Cavanaugh. She had needed him so much in those dark days following her mother's death.

She hadn't been brave enough to go through with it and leave the village, so she had convinced herself that it would be too hard to track him down.

Eloise chastised herself for making excuses. When she had finally left the pride in order to bring him back, it had taken her two years, but she had found him. She closed her eyes and pressed her forehead against her bare knees. The thought that she might have been with him for at least the last three years, living in London and maybe working at the same nightclub, ran on repeat in her head.

She should have gone after him that snowy morning and not listened to her mother.

She drew in a slow breath, lifted her head, and exhaled it. There was little point in wondering what might have been and playing the *should have* game. Cavanaugh should have done a lot of things differently if he truly had feelings for her too, but he hadn't. Both of them were at fault for what had happened, back then and even now.

He had sprung something huge on her, telling her that he had left because he couldn't bear seeing her drift away from him.

She hadn't reacted in the smoothest way.

Gods. Now he was standing on a ledge several hundred metres up the side of a mountain and no doubt cursing her name.

She had to speak with him.

Eloise shifted onto her hands and knees, and crawled towards the narrow exit of the cave. She slowed as his bare feet came into view, her heart beginning a slow, steady thump against her chest. She had to do this. She pushed onwards and came out onto the ledge behind him.

He whirled to face her and frowned. "Go back inside. You'll freeze out here."

She had forgotten that she was only dressed in her underwear, but she wasn't going to let the cold deter her.

Even if it was freezing.

Wind whipped across the wall of rock, battering her and loosening strands of her dark hair. It played in Cavanaugh's too, tousling the silver-white tufts, and plastered his dark grey trousers to his legs.

Eloise kneeled and rubbed her arms. "I'm sorry."

He stared at her, the question in his gaze asking whether she had come out into the frigid cold just to apologise again or whether there was anything else she had to say.

She looked out at the valley and everything she had wanted to say to Cavanaugh fled her lips. Normally, the view was spectacular, a lush green valley that followed the river as it snaked down through the mountains. The tops of those mountains were grey rock tipped with dazzling white snow. Not today.

Today heavy grey clouds hid their peaks and she couldn't make out the valley beyond a few hundred metres below her.

Snow swallowed it.

The first few flakes drifted down and settled on the ledge, and on her bare skin, melting on contact.

This wasn't good. A snowstorm would keep them trapped in the shelter, unable to continue their climb until it had blown over and the wind had swept the snow and ice off the rock face.

Cavanaugh stared out towards the storm as it slowly closed in on them. "We wouldn't make it."

Had he been reading her mind? She had been on the verge of saying they had to leave now.

She looked up at the thick clouds that were already overhead. "We have to try... if we don't..."

"I know what happens if we don't," he said, a sharp edge to his deep voice. "I know what happens if we do, too. It's over two hundred metres to the top. It would take too long to climb that far. It's better we're not caught in the open when it hits."

She knew that but she didn't care. The pride were relying on her and she was so close to having Cavanaugh back with them.

The quiet voice in her heart said that she didn't care about that or the pride. She cared about Cavanaugh. She had already messed up once on the climb and he had somehow saved her. If she messed up again, in the middle of a snowstorm, she might end up killing both of them.

White flakes swirled on the wind, steadily drifting down towards her.

"Back inside," Cavanaugh said and she didn't argue with him.

Eloise turned around and crawled back into the cave. He followed her and a blush burned up her cheeks when she realised she was giving him a free show, flashing her backside at him. She hastily got onto her feet on the other side of the wall, scurrying away from him.

He made it through the entrance, rose onto his feet and went for his pack. He crouched beside it, pulled out some protein bars, clothing and other items, and then stood and carried the pack towards the door, together with hers. The snow was already creeping inside. Cavanaugh stopped it by wedging their backpacks across the bottom of the entrance, sealing the lower half of the gap.

"That should keep us warmer." He turned back towards her and met her eyes before averting his down to his bare feet. "We might have to share body heat again… if you can bring yourself to be near a monster."

"Cavanaugh," Eloise snapped and his grey eyes leaped to hers. "I never said you were a monster… just… it hurt that you stayed away. It hurt that one day we were best friends and the next you were acting like a stranger."

"Gods, Eloise…" He scrubbed his left hand over his silver-white hair. "I didn't want it to be like that… but what was I meant to do?"

Talk to her. He was meant to talk to her. She would have listened to him and she might not have spent years believing she had meant nothing to him.

She lowered her gaze back to her feet. It was cold and she didn't have the energy to think, let alone argue with him. She trudged to the clothes she had spotted on the floor and picked up her beige trousers. They were damp. So was her top.

"Here." Cavanaugh rounded her, stooped and scooped up his long sleeve black thermal top. He offered it to her. "I meant to lay your clothes out to dry but I forgot."

Because he had been focused on warming her.

"You could have talked to me," she whispered and took the top from him, ignoring the confused crinkle of his brow. He knew damned well that she wasn't talking about yesterday when she had been unconscious. She was talking about a decade ago. She lifted the top to her nose.

It smelled of Cavanaugh.

Gods, she wanted to rub it all over herself.

She tamped down that feline urge and put it on.

"What could I have said?" Cavanaugh stepped into her, his hands claiming her hips, guiding her backwards towards the sleeping bags.

She stared up into his grey eyes, lost in them, feeling as if he was beating down her defences all over again. Every time she reconstructed them, he went to war again, tearing them down. His eyes darted between hers and his silver eyebrows furrowed.

"Tell me, Eloise," he husked. "If I had told you that I wanted you, what would you have done?"

She dragged her eyes away from his, dropping them to his bare chest. "I don't know."

"You don't know," he echoed and she swallowed hard and nodded. He sighed. "You don't know because there is no answer where we get what we want… is there?"

He released her and stepped back, his eyes lowering to his feet as hers rose to his.

He looked vulnerable, a male stripped of his power and strength, one who was breaking inside. She didn't like it. It filled her with a need to step towards him and slide her arms around his neck, bringing his lips down to hers for a kiss that would relay all of her feelings for him and chase away his pain.

"There is no way for me to have you… not the way I want you." He scrubbed his hand around the back of his neck and closed his eyes. "If I had gone to you back then and told you that I wanted you, it wouldn't have changed a thing… just as it doesn't change a thing now. It doesn't change my status or the things I did."

She wished he hadn't said that last part. The things he had done. A brief flash of the pride females blasted across her eyes and she shut them, wishing she could shut out the images too. They refused to go away.

"I never wanted this," he whispered.

Eloise opened her eyes and looked at him. "What did you want?"

He lifted his gaze to hers, silver glowing around his dark pupils.

"You."

CHAPTER 10

Gods help her, but when Cavanaugh looked at her like that, with desire darkening his grey eyes but making them burn at the same time, she lost all of her will to resist him.

Eloise had stepped into his arms, claimed his shoulders and pulled him down to her before she could even consider what she was doing. She fused her mouth with his in a hard kiss, one born of the need blazing through her, hunger that had been building from the moment she had set eyes on him in London. She could no longer deny it. She was surprised she had made it this far without surrendering to it.

The wind howled across the mountain and the scent of snow grew thicker, but she didn't care. She didn't feel the cold as Cavanaugh's hands clamped down on her hips and he slowly drew her against him. She felt only the scorching heat of the desire that burned within her heart and her body, a need and hunger that only he could satisfy.

Tomorrow was for regrets.

Today was for living.

His tongue stroked the seam of her lips and she opened for him, earning a low husky growl as her reward for complying with his demands. She angled her head and tangled her tongue with his, the taste of him taking her back to that night a decade ago, when she had given herself to him and he had given himself to her. She moaned and clutched his shoulders, pressing her nails in as she clung to him, riding the storm that swirled in her veins and blasted through her, passion that burned hotter than it had back then.

It consumed her and she could only surrender herself to it, to the intoxicating press of his fingers against her bare hips and the fierce demand of his lips on hers. He groaned and slid one hand around to the small of her back, pinning her against him. It wasn't enough for her. She broke free, ignored his growl as it echoed around the small low-lit cave, and cut it off when she tugged his top back off over her head and tossed it away from her. Her bra followed it and he moaned, his gaze dropping to hungrily devour what she offered.

"Eloise," he murmured and grabbed her arm, dragging her back to him. His mouth claimed hers again, a wild edge to his kiss that told her she wasn't the only one lost in the moment, no longer in control of themselves.

She needed more than his kiss though.

She needed all of him.

Eloise stroked her fingers down his chest and stomach, moaning into his mouth as his muscles tensed, sending a fiery shiver bolting through her and all of the fire in her veins rushing to her belly. She made swift work of his trouser buttons as her lips clashed with his, their tongues duelling. When the last button gave way, his cock sprang free and she groaned again as she rubbed her palm down the length of it, from the crown to his balls.

Cavanaugh shuddered and moaned, his big body quaking against hers. His shaft jerked in her hand and she stroked it again, teasing him with the leisurely and light caress. He seized hold of her hips and guided her backwards, but she stopped him in his tracks by cupping his balls, rolling them in her fingers. His lips froze against hers, his breathing ragged as she stroked him again, circling his length with her fingers and slowly gliding up and down. He was bigger than she remembered, hot and heavy in her hand. She rubbed her thumb over the crown, smearing the pearl of moisture into his soft skin.

He groaned and his fingers tensed against her hips. He liked that.

She smiled and kissed him as she stroked him, teasing him by alternating between light and slow, and hard and fast. He breathed hard against her lips between kisses, the scent of his arousal heavy in the cold air. She moaned at the same time as he did as he began walking with her again, inching her back towards the sleeping bags.

Eloise stopped him this time by turning with him, and seemed to surprise him by backing him towards the warm blankets, because he groaned low and long, a pained look on his face.

She pressed down on his shoulders and he obeyed, sitting on the sleeping bags and staring up at her, his cock jerking against his stomach. She slipped her fingers into the sides of her knickers and slowly eased them down her thighs, her eyes never leaving his.

"Eloise," he whispered, his breathing coming faster and his pupils gobbling up his silver irises.

He palmed his length, the sight so sensual and wicked that it tore a moan from her. He did it again, his big hand wrapping around it this time, stroking himself as she undressed for him. She rubbed her thighs together and moaned as she realised how slick she was already, hungry for him. His eyes darkened and he drew a deep breath, his gaze turning hooded. He could smell her desire just as she could smell his. There was no denying that she wanted this and so did he.

And there would be no denying her either.

He was going to do things her way or not at all.

She kicked her knickers aside and walked towards him. His throat worked on a hard swallow, his sexy Adam's apple dipping beneath the fine layer of silver stubble that coated his jaw and neck. She kneeled when she reached the blanket, placing one leg on either side of his and straddling them.

He reached for her.

She denied him and ran her hands up his thighs, to the top of his grey trousers. She tugged them down, not stopping until they were at his knees, and then ran her hands back up his legs, over the toned muscles of his thighs. They quivered beneath her touch.

Eloise shuffled closer to him and settled herself on his thighs. She pressed her hands to his chest, pinning him against the rock wall, and kissed him again. He growled into her mouth, seizing control of the kiss in an instant, his hands questing over her thighs. She expected him to shift them around to her bottom and draw her against him.

He did the opposite.

He slipped his hands between her legs and kept travelling upwards, to their apex, where he swept them over the top of her thighs. She moaned and kissed him harder, aching to have him touch her most private place. She needed his hands on her. She flexed her hips, eliciting a low moan from him, and his thumbs brushed her inner thighs again, stroking the neat curls covering her mound.

"Cavanaugh," she whispered, willing to give him what he wanted if he would then give her what she needed.

He smiled against her mouth and kissed her as he dipped his hands between her thighs and stroked her wet folds. She moaned at the same time as he did, the feel of his cool fingers against her overheating flesh sending stars shooting through her.

He angled his hand and rubbed her with the pads of two fingers, tearing moan after moan from her lips as she tried to resist rocking her hips. She tensed her muscles and shuddered as she stepped dangerously close to the edge of bliss. It was hard to force herself to relax again but she managed it as she kissed him, using all of her willpower to stop herself from finding release. She wanted him inside her when it happened.

She needed him inside her again.

She seized his hands and pinned them to the wall on either side of his head. He moaned, the sound low and wicked, sending heat curling through her. She had never been assertive in the times they had been together. She had been too caught up in his primal heat to do anything but submit to him.

Now he would submit to her.

Eloise drew back and he stared at her, his grey gaze hooded, his sensual lips rosy from her kiss. He looked more satisfied now than he had ever looked back then, and she hadn't even brought him to climax yet. She could change that.

She rose onto her knees and pressed harder against his wrists when he tried to move them. His eyes widened and then narrowed, setting her on fire. He approved of this side of her. He wanted to submit to her. Gods, just the thought of Cavanaugh at her mercy had her on the verge of finding release.

He groaned when she brought them into contact, rubbing her slick heat up and down his rigid length, and tipped his head back into the wall, a look of agony crossing his handsome face. She would put him out of his misery, because she couldn't take the teasing either, not this time.

She rocked her hips upwards, rising higher on her knees at the same time, until the blunt head of his cock pressed into her aroused nub. She angled her body into his, caught the crown of his length and pressed downwards, so it slipped down towards where she needed him.

A moan escaped her when he nudged against her entrance.

Eloise shifted her hands in his, interlinking their fingers but keeping his hands pinned to the wall. She screwed her face up, pressing her forehead against Cavanaugh's, their panted breaths mingling as she slowly eased down onto his cock, taking him inch by delicious inch into her wet heat. He half-moaned half-growled as the tip of him struck her deepest point and she rotated her hips, making sure he was in as far as he could go.

"Eloise," he whispered and she gave him what he wanted.

She clutched his hands and kissed him as she rode him, long and fast thrusts that left no part of her untouched by him. He rocked his hips, countering her, thrusting up each time she drove down and pulling away whenever she rose off him again. She moaned into his mouth, lost in the bliss tripping through her as his cock filled her, stretching and completing her. Gods, it had never been like this.

She had never dreamed it could be like this.

He pressed his fingers into the backs of her hands and grunted as he kissed her, thrusting deep into her, sending her soaring out of her mind. She quickened her pace, breathing hard between each frantic clash of their lips and fierce meeting of their bodies. Each brush of his body across her sensitive nub sent waves of tingles spreading through her, upwards to her belly where they swirled together, steadily building towards a crescendo.

She released his hands, gripped his shoulders and groaned as she rode him, desperately seeking release. He grasped her backside and seized control, helping her maintain a ferocious pace as he drove every inch of his cock into her, taking her harder.

"Eloise," he grunted and she pressed her cheek against his, unable to do anything but moan as she soared higher, spiralling upwards, almost within reach of her climax.

He thrust deeper and faster and she cried out as her body slammed against his and she shattered into a thousand pieces, fire blazing through her bones and shimmering over her thighs and up her belly. She clutched his shoulders and moaned with each hard meeting of their hips as he thrust more frantically, his forehead pressed against her cheek and his breath hot on her neck.

"Gods," he groaned and then growled. It rolled into a roar as he shoved her down, pinning her onto him as he spilled himself inside her, throbbing and sending aftershocks of pleasure rippling through her.

His grip on her slowly loosened as he breathed hard, out of sync with her own panted gasps for air.

Eloise sagged against him, struggling to bring herself down. Her bones had turned to rubber and her body felt too heavy to move. He wrapped his arms around her and she pressed her cheek to his shoulder, too tired to move from his lap or untangle their bodies. She liked the feel of him inside her as tiny tremors ran through him and he slowly softened, spent from their lovemaking.

The wind howled across the mouth of the cave again.

Eloise still didn't care.

She could regret everything tomorrow.

Today she was going to live.

She was going to seize this moment with Cavanaugh.

Even when she knew in her heart that he was right.

There was no way for them to get what they wanted.

There would be no forever after for them.

CHAPTER 11

Cavanaugh lay propped up on his right elbow with Eloise tucked against him, watching her as she dozed beneath the blanket with him. His beautiful, and surprising, fated female. He had wanted her to initiate things between them, but he hadn't anticipated what had followed. His Eloise had grown stronger and more courageous. He wanted to be proud of her because of that, but in his heart he feared that her new courage and strength was the result of all the pain and suffering she had endured.

He softly stroked a rogue strand of her wavy dark hair from her forehead, smoothing it into the rest, and sighed as he looked at her.

He hadn't wanted to argue with her, but he was glad that some things were out in the open now and they could find a way to move past them. He needed to find the way to tell her everything else he had wanted to say too. His courage had failed him though, and he had only managed to let her know that he wanted her and that was the reason he had left. She had every right to be angry with him for how he had handled everything, but he hoped that she could forgive him.

Could she?

If he told her that she was his mate, what would she say?

Would she be happy? Or would she be sad because his status stood between them and a bond that was both special and precious?

Most snow leopards never found their mates.

Unlike other shifter species, a snow leopard's fated mate was always another snow leopard. With their numbers dwindling, their long life spans and their prides spread across the world, it was hard to find their fated mate. Most of his kind found love without finding their mate, settling down to produce offspring and ensure the future of their race. Others scoured the Earth for their fated one, driven by a relentless need to find their other half. Even if a snow leopard travelled to all the prides, there was no guarantee their mate was with one. There was a high chance their mate would be born long after their visit.

But Cavanaugh had found his.

She lay in his arms.

And she had stolen his heart long before he had ever realised that she was his fated mate.

"Why are you staring at me?" she murmured sleepily and yawned. "I can feel you staring."

"I was thinking." He dropped a kiss on her cheek.

"About what?" She cracked her eyes open and squinted at him, the start of a smile curving her rosy lips.

"How beautiful you are."

She shoved him in his chest, making him jerk backwards, and scowled. She thought he was joking. Never. In the short period they had been together as more than friends, he had never told her enough times that she was beautiful. He meant to make up for it now. He meant to make up for a lot of things he had done wrong.

"I was." He let her see the truth in his eyes as he looked at her, thinking about how beautiful she was, with her honey-coloured eyes, her sweet heart-shaped lips, impish button nose and her hair mussed from making love with him, and her bare body tucked close to his.

"Not just about how beautiful I apparently am." She cast a pointed look down between them and then looked back into his eyes.

Cavanaugh shrugged. "Call it evidence of how your beauty affects me."

He caught her right hand and brought it down between them, settling it over his aching hard shaft.

When he released her, she took her hand away, and he frowned and pouted. She rolled onto her back, propped herself up on her elbows and looked down the length of their bodies, towards the cave entrance, her eyes narrowing. He could feel her focus sharpening, her senses growing stronger as she honed them on the world outside.

Cavanaugh pressed a kiss to her bare left shoulder. "It's still snowing."

She huffed and looked across at him. "Your senses always were better than mine."

Because he was male, and because whenever he was around her, he was on high alert, everything sharpened and focused.

So he could protect her.

But he had failed to do that.

He eased his left hand under her right one, drew it up off the covers and rubbed his thumb over the scars on her wrist. She stilled and he sensed the trickle of fear that ran through her. She didn't want him to ask about them, but he needed to know.

"What happened here?" he whispered, keeping his eyes locked on her wrist so she didn't feel pressurised into telling him straight away. He had all the time in the world.

Neither of them were going anywhere for a while, not until the storm had abated and the winds had cleared the path up the cliff face.

It was just the two of them, trapped in a small cave, together again at last.

"Stellan punishes any he thinks are working behind his back." Her voice was quiet and distant, and he could sense the pain in her, the hurt he was causing her by asking her to remember the terrible things that had happened to her.

Things he should have been there to stop from happening.

He should have been there to protect her.

"Were you working behind his back?" Cavanaugh ran his thumb over the scars. They had been made by ropes, and looked as if it hadn't been just one occasion when she had been bound and punished.

She shook her head.

"Then why did he punish you?" Dread settled in his stomach the second he finished his question, churning it until it burned and fire sprinted through his veins, chasing back the ice that had shot through them. He closed his eyes and gripped her slender wrist. "Because of me. He punished you because of me."

She didn't answer him. She didn't need to. Silence stretched between them, thick with the things she didn't dare to voice. Stellan had known of their relationship and he had targeted her because of it.

"Gods, I'm sorry, Eloise," Cavanaugh whispered and brought her hand to his lips and pressed a kiss to her wrist.

He rested his lips against her warm skin, breathing her in, using her sweet scent to calm himself and reassure himself that whatever had happened to her, she was safe now. He would never allow anything to happen to her, never again.

"It wasn't your fault." Her voice was as quiet as his own, raspy with the emotions that poured from her and into him through where they touched and the threads that tied them together.

He had always felt a deep connection to her, a sense that they were bound in some way, and he hadn't been surprised when his instincts had finally told him that she was his fated one. The connection he felt to her, and was sure she felt to him, was that uninitiated bond at work. When they finally mated, it would awaken to its full potential, linking them physically and emotionally, giving them the ability to sense each other over great distances, and to know when the other was hurt or in danger.

"It was… I should have been there, Eloise. I can't forgive myself for failing you." He drew in another deep breath and then started when she shifted her right hand in his and cupped his left cheek.

She was soft and warm against him, too wonderful for him to bear as she gently held his face, a wealth of emotions in her light caress. They undid him, ripping down the strength he had been clinging to for years, leaving him weak and vulnerable, and at her mercy.

"I'm not saying that what you did was right, because there isn't a minute that goes by where I don't wish you had taken me with you, but I know now why you did it. I understand, Cavanaugh, and I forgive you for it." She smiled when he opened his eyes, seeking the truth in hers. They shone at him, filled with the forgiveness she had spoken of and an overwhelming amount of affection. He clasped her hand to his face and her smile widened, softening at the same time, giving him the comfort he craved.

When that smile began to fade, and her feelings altered course, a fierce need to stop her from talking welled up inside him, because he knew the direction she was about to take their conversation in and he didn't want her to talk about what lay ahead of them.

He wanted to savour this moment with her and pretend the rest of the world didn't exist. Here in this cave, with her, he wasn't the alpha of a pride. He was only her Cavanaugh, and that was all he had ever wanted to be.

Hers.

Cavanaugh wrapped his fingers around her wrist and moved his arm, bringing hers over his left shoulder and drawing her closer to him. His gaze fell to her mouth, to the tempting sensual curves of her lips, and he almost groaned when her tongue poked out, sweeping across them, an invitation he wouldn't turn down.

He leaned towards her, rolled her onto her back and captured her lips with his, eliciting a soft moan from her that had him hardening again and instantly hungry for more. He managed to keep the kiss light and slow, not wanting to rush this time.

He wanted this moment to last forever.

He wanted to shower her with the love that beat in his heart for her.

Cavanaugh released her wrist and she wrapped her arms around his neck, her kiss as soft as his, bare sweeps of her lips across his. They tingled in response, each caress making him feel lighter inside, until he felt sure that they were floating and the world around them fell away. Her breasts pressed against his bare chest, her soft body cushioning his. He lifted his left leg over her, nestling it between her thighs. She moaned as his thigh settled against her mound and his hard length pressed against her hip.

Her kiss grew more demanding and he surrendered to it but refused to let her turn it as wild as it had been when they had last made love.

She skimmed her hands over his shoulders and pressed her short nails in as he kissed down her jaw, following the line of it to her neck. She tilted her head to one side, giving him access to her throat, and he growled as he kissed and licked it, a primal need awakening inside him. He kissed towards the back of her neck, pulling her hair away from it with his right hand and exposing it. She moaned and arched against him as he tongued her nape, a slave to his need to taste her there.

To sink his fangs into that soft flesh and pin her while he mated with her.

"Cavanaugh," she whispered breathlessly, her own need slamming through him, driving him into surrendering to his urge to bite her.

He breathed hard, fighting it, unwilling to give in to it when everything was still up in the air and she was unaware that he was her mate. He couldn't force a bond on her, not when she believed he was going to return to being the pride alpha, a role that would see them separated again.

He licked her nape one last time and reluctantly dragged himself away, kissing down over her shoulder towards her breasts instead. They were as far as he could go with his mouth while remaining inside the covers. As much as he wanted to kiss between her thighs, tasting the arousal he stirred within her, he had to content himself with kissing and suckling her breasts. Night had fallen and the temperature had dropped dramatically. Kissing between her thighs meant stripping open the double sleeping bag, and he didn't want her to get a chill.

It wouldn't do much for him either, not when some parts of the male anatomy didn't take kindly to frigid temperatures.

His cock jerked and he groaned as he kissed her breasts, swirling his tongue around her left nipple. He would have it somewhere hot and moist soon enough, nice and warm.

Eloise moaned as he danced the fingers of his left hand down over her belly, feeling it flutter beneath them, and he joined her with a groan of his own as she edged her thighs apart, inviting him in.

He settled his palm over her mound and slipped two fingers between her plush petals, and groaned again as he felt how wet she was already, eager for him. His cock throbbed again, nudging against her leg, and he sucked her nipple harder, tugging on it as his desire got the better of him.

She tipped her head back and unleashed a sweet cry of pleasure as her hands fumbled with his shoulders and his head. She twisted her fingers into his hair and clutched him to her as she panted, her breaths coming quicker as he stroked her aroused nub, swirling his fingers around it at the same time as he suckled her nipple. The scent of her desire filled his senses, awakening every male and primal instinct. They demanded that he satisfy his female.

He obeyed.

He slid his left hand lower, seeking her centre, and she cried out again as he eased two fingers into her sheath. He groaned against her breast as he pumped her, feeling her slick heat encasing him. Gods, he wanted to be in there, buried deep, filling her and feeling her gripping him.

"Cavanaugh." His name falling from her lips as a plea shattered his restraint.

He pulled his fingers free of her and wedged himself between her thighs. She moaned and ran her hands down his back, pressing her fingers into his spine above his bottom and bringing him down against her. He shuddered as his hard shaft pressed against her wetness, her heat scalding him.

"Eloise," he whispered and braced himself on his hands above her, one either side of her head.

Her honey-coloured eyes met his, desire darkening them, passion and need that he could satisfy. His female needed.

She needed him.

Her right hand skimmed around his hip and he followed her silent command, easing back and allowing her to wrap her fingers around him. He grunted when she brushed her thumb over the crown, teasing him, and she smiled and slowly guided him downwards.

Cavanaugh held his breath.

She eased the tip of his cock into her and he groaned in time with her as he slid forwards, driving himself into her hot tight sheath. She gripped him hard, her body clenching around his, ripping a grunt from him that she smiled at again.

He moved his arms to either side of her ribs, dropped onto his elbows and wiped the smile off her face by sliding deeper still, filling her completely. Her lips parted and he swooped on them, swallowing her moan as he began to thrust, long leisurely strokes that had him almost coming free of her before he eased back inside.

She raised her hips, allowing him to slide even deeper, so he left no part of her untouched as he drove into her.

He grasped her hip with one hand to support her and kissed her as he slowly pumped into her, battling his need and every urge that commanded him to go faster and harder.

Not this time.

This time he was going to make love with her for the first time.

The very first time in his life.

It was so much more than he had imagined it could be. Every experience he had, it had happened with her, and it had always been frenetic, a passionate and wild coupling.

He had thought it couldn't get better than that.

He had been wrong.

Moving inside her like this, slow and unhurried, his mouth fused with hers in a tender kiss, rocked his world and shook him to his core. More than their bodies were linked. They were joined in every way, from their bodies to their hearts and right down to their souls.

She moaned beneath him, her fingers tangling in his hair, her kiss as soft as his own. Her feelings flowed into him, mingling with his, echoing them and heightening how good everything felt. Every plunge of his cock into her and every withdraw, every sweep of her tongue across his lips or fusing of their mouths, all of it shook him, until he felt sure he was dreaming, experiencing a vivid fantasy that wasn't really possible in real life.

"Cavanaugh," she murmured against his lips and he felt the need building within her as she clenched him, flexing her body around his. Her scent and her feelings spoke to his instincts, warning that she was close.

He clutched her hip and drove deeper as he kissed her harder, steadily building them towards a crescendo. She moaned and writhed, her need pounding through him. He gave her what she needed, a willing slave for her, consumed by his need to satisfy his female. She cried out as he pumped her harder, curling his hips to strike her deepest point and her sweetest spot.

She broke away from his mouth and pressed her forehead against his, clinging to him as he thrust into her. Her breathless moans were music to his ears and he closed his eyes and grunted as his balls drew up, his cock growing thicker as release coiled at its base.

His breathing turned ragged, unsteady gasps that she matched as she flexed her body around his, seeking her release. Her body tensed, going rigid beneath him, and he dropped his lips back to hers and swallowed her cry in a kiss as she climaxed, quivering and trembling around him, her thighs shaking against his hips.

He screwed his face up and grunted as his own release blasted through him and his cock pulsed and throbbed hard, shooting hot jets of his seed into her welcoming body. He clumsily kissed her as his climax swept through him, his entire body quaking from it.

Eloise kissed him softly, slowly bringing him down, luring him back to Earth with her. He settled against her and rolled over, bringing her on top of him so he didn't crush her with his weight. She rested her head against his chest. He could feel her heart racing, thundering as his was, and he could feel her trembling too as he ran his hands up and down her spine, savouring how good it felt to be with her like this.

He closed his eyes and breathed out a sigh as he wrapped his arms around her and held her pinned to his chest.

He would have this forever.

Nothing would stand in his way.

Eloise would be his mate.

CHAPTER 12

Cavanaugh found a hold in the thick snow and hauled himself up onto the plateau above the sheer cliff, rolled into the snow, and grabbed hold of the rope attached to his harness. He braced his boots against a boulder near the edge of the plateau, made sure the rope ran over one of his boots to stop it from chafing on the rocks, and began to pull. He easily took Eloise's slender weight, steadily pulling her up the cliff face with the rope.

Her hands appeared first, red from the cold, groping around in the snow. He looped the rope around his left arm, making sure it wouldn't slip from his grip and holding her steady, and then reached out with his right arm, stretching for her. He snagged her right wrist and she twisted her hand and grabbed onto his wrist, locking them together.

He leaned backwards and hauled her up, pulling her over the edge and onto the plateau with him. She slumped face first on the snow, breathing hard, and he pulled her closer. Snow built up around her shoulders and against her face and she scowled at him. She could be angry about the cold all she wanted. All he cared about was making sure that she was away from the edge and safe before she relaxed and took a break.

The climb had been hard, the freezing temperatures turning what remained of the snow into ice, making it difficult to get a good grip on the rocks and handholds.

He had come close to slipping at one point, his left boot skidding off a small ledge he had thought would be a safe foothold. Eloise had snapped at him, berating him for almost five minutes after he had managed to save himself and stop himself from plummeting to a grisly death with her.

He smiled fondly at the memory.

She hadn't been angry with him. She had been worried and it had come out in the form of reprimanding him.

"What is with that stupid smile?" She huffed and got onto her hands and knees, and then sat up, rubbing her hands together and blowing on them.

He grinned and sat up. "Nothing. Just thinking about how worried about me you were back there."

She playfully punched him on the arm. "I had every damned right to be worried. You almost killed us."

Cavanaugh caught her fist when she went to hit him again and kissed it before smoothing his fingers over it, concern growing inside him as he saw just how red her fingers were.

"Come on, you need to get warmed up." He shoved onto his feet and pulled her onto hers, and kept hold of her as he led her a few metres back from the edge, to a safer place.

He released her and drew in deep breaths, slowing his heart as it pounded from the exertion of the climb. Mountains rose above them still, tall cragged and forbidding white peaks. They were only two-thirds of the way up them, with the forest in the valley and the smaller mountains stretching below him like a beautiful painting, more fantasy than reality.

He had forgotten how stunning this place was. The land of his people.

No humans ventured here. Only his shifter kin and the real snow leopards. Even the tigers that had made a home at altitude didn't climb this high. The air was thin and cold, burning his lungs. His head ached already. It would take a day at the least to become acclimatised to the higher altitude and the thinner air. Until it happened, he needed to keep away from the village. He was in no position to fight. He would be out of breath in seconds, and dizzy within minutes, and liable to pass out from the exertion and strain on his body.

He undid the harness around his waist and stepped out of it, leaving it on the packed snow, and removed his pack.

Eloise slipped her backpack off and opened it. She stuffed her harness into it, together with his and the rope, and pulled out the thick fleece she had worn in the forest and a lightweight white wind-and-waterproof jacket. He meant to get his gear out too, but could only stare at her as she quickly stripped off her wet thermal top, flashing her black bra, and replaced it with a dry one. When she put her stone fleece on, Cavanaugh set about changing.

He pulled his thermal off over his head and slowed as he felt her watching him, her gaze roaming his body, heating him wherever it touched. He flashed her a smile as he dumped the damp top on his pack. She glanced away but her gaze crept back to him as he pulled out a fresh long sleeve black thermal top and straightened to put it on. He let her get another good long look at his body as he slipped his arms into the top and then pulled it down.

The dark grey fleece followed it, and then his lighter grey waterproof jacket. With his top half already warming up, he set about dealing with his bottom half. He pulled out a pair of white waterproof trousers for Eloise and one for himself. She took the small pouch that contained the trousers from him and set it down on her pack, a miserable look on her face.

He didn't exactly relish the thought of getting his tackle out in the freezing temperatures either, but there was little point in putting the weatherproof trousers on over wet clothing.

She spread her wet thermal top on the snow, removed her boots, and stepped onto the top. He did the same with his, using it as a barrier to keep the snow off his new dry clothing. He toed his boots off and quickly changed from his dark grey trousers into a lighter grey pair, pulled his weatherproof trousers on over the top of them, and then changed his socks one at a time, switching them for thick thermal wool ones and putting each foot back into his boots straight away so they didn't get wet.

He tossed a pair of socks to Eloise. She nodded her thanks and put on her white weatherproof trousers over the top of her other ones, swiftly changed socks and jammed her feet back into her boots.

Cavanaugh bent and tucked his grey trousers into his boots before tying them. He smoothed the weatherproof trousers down over the top and tugged the elastic that ran around their inner layer, pushing the toggle down to make sure they were snug against the tops of his boots. No snow getting in that way.

Eloise straightened and rubbed her hands together between packing away her damp top and trousers. He shoved his kit back into his bag and then took the thermal gloves from the front pocket. He handed the smaller pair to Eloise.

She stared at them and then at him.

He shrugged and smiled. "You always get cold hands."

And she always forgot her gloves.

"Thanks." She smiled back at him and pulled them on, a brief flicker of bliss crossing her pretty face as she flexed her fingers.

That flicker became a full on burst that shone in a smile that hit him straight in the heart when he held out a white woollen hat to her.

She snatched it from him, purred lovingly as she stroked the fluffy white lining inside the hat, and then put it on and beamed at him. He had never seen her so happy. If he had known the way to her heart was simple but thoughtful gifts like gloves and hats, he would have showered her with them all those years ago.

"Where's yours?" She frowned as she stroked the hat over her temples.

"As I recall, I'm not the one who always complained about how their ears were going to freeze and fall off." That earned him a playful glare.

Gods, he really had missed her.

He had her back now though, but he feared it wouldn't last. Every step closer they took to the village was one that would slowly increase the distance between them again, even when he didn't want that to happen. He didn't want to lose her again. He wanted her to stay like this, filled with smiles, every meeting of their eyes telling him that she felt something for him.

He finished with his pack and put it on, tightening the straps over his shoulders. "We should head off. It's a long trek to the next shelter and I want to be there by nightfall."

They had agreed they would rest overnight in another small cave at the base of one of the mountains halfway between the cliff and the village, and continue in the morning. It was too dangerous to head on from that point tonight because they would have to cross the snowfields to the other side of the valley. Crossing in the darkness would be suicide.

They needed the overnight stop for another reason too. It would give them both time to acclimatise and prepare.

Eloise gave him a look that said she still wanted to make him go straight to the village, but thankfully didn't put voice to that desire. He knew she didn't want him to fight again and that was the sole reason she wanted him to reach the village before he lost his title as alpha.

They had argued about it in the cave halfway up the climb before leaving it and she had confessed it to him. She had confessed something else too, but without words. He had seen in her eyes and felt in her that taking him back to the pride was hurting her. Part of her didn't want to bring him back. He was glad of that. It told him how she felt about him and gave him courage and hope that he might have done enough to win her heart and her as his mate.

He had reassured her that he would do all in his power to avoid a fight, but Stellan might not be as accommodating. Stellan would want to defend his claim to the pride.

She had been away from the mountain now. She knew how much the change in altitude could affect their bodies because it was affecting her just as it was him.

She knew he would be in danger if he had to fight.

It had been enough to get her to agree to stopping overnight to rest and acclimatise.

Eloise put her backpack on and he looked across the valley ahead of them. Wind blew down it, stirring the snow. The valley snaked between two of the largest mountains, immense dangerous peaks that speared the sky. All they had to do was follow that valley and they would come to the village, but the path across the basin was treacherous, riddled with crevasses. They could easily place a foot wrong and slip into one.

"We'll take the higher path," Cavanaugh said and she looked back at him. He didn't look at her. His gaze remained fixed on charting the path that followed the side of the mountain to his left, or where it should be beneath the snow. If they were lucky, the local snow leopards would have used it recently, outlining it for them.

If they weren't, it would be tough going, but it was still better than taking the path across the valley.

He hadn't been across it in five years, and Eloise hadn't traversed it in two. In that time, the crevasses could have shifted away from where they knew them to be and they might walk straight into one that hadn't been there before. Even if they made it across the valley basin, they would still need to make a second crossing to reach the village. Another valley intersected the mountains on the right hand side of this one.

It was best they stayed on the higher path until the point where it dropped down into the valley and crossed the snowfields there. They were more stable and it was a much shorter crossing.

He glanced at Eloise and she nodded.

Cavanaugh took hold of her right hand, slipping his fingers between hers, and started walking towards the base of the mountain. He kept his gaze on the path ahead of him, scouring the eye-numbing white snow for any signs the ground beneath might not be solid.

It didn't take long for them to come across a trail. He crouched and touched the wide paw prints. Snow leopards had trekked in both directions along it. His eyes followed the path as it curved off to his right and he smiled as he saw it curled around and headed towards the mountain ahead of him.

He rose onto his feet and followed the animal trail, his eyes still locked on the snow and checking it for signs of danger.

When the path led them up the side of the mountain, he released Eloise so she could walk behind him and began to relax again and take in his surroundings. The valley and mountains looked beautiful against the bright blue sky, a sharp contrast that took his breath away.

Eloise fell in behind him, her scent swirling around him together with the sharp tang of snow. He wanted her beside him, but the path was narrow, snaking up and down as it followed the side of the mountain above the valley floor.

Cavanaugh stared ahead of them, tracking the path at first, and then looking beyond the far end of the mountain. The village stood there, miles away but drawing ever closer. He drew in a deep breath to quell his nerves. He still wasn't sure what he was heading into and it was time he found out.

"How many men does Stellan have on his side?" he said, keeping his voice down so he didn't disturb the thick snow above him on the mountain. The last thing he needed was an avalanche. They were common, particularly at this time of year when the weather was warming during the day.

"Five males who are always with him. At least another six who might fight on his side."

Cavanaugh huffed. That was most of the males in the village then. Stellan must have won them over through brute force, showing them how powerful he was so they would think twice about rising up against him.

"What about August?" He looked back at Eloise, needing to see in her eyes whether his cousin had pledged himself to Stellan.

She shook her head. "He isn't with Stellan… but Stellan keeps a close eye on him."

Cavanaugh had expected as much. August was the next in Cavanaugh's bloodline, the son of his father's brother. Cavanaugh's father had only managed to produce two male heirs in his time as alpha. Normally, if Cavanaugh died as things were, outside of a fight against a challenger and while he was still the alpha but without any heirs of his own, the pride would pass to his younger brother, Harbin.

But Harbin had been exiled by their father twenty years ago.

Harbin had been hot-headed and had never seen eye to eye with their father. It had all come to a head when his brother had fallen in with a woman in a sleazy bar, spilling shit to her that he should have kept to himself.

Harbin had tried to impress her by telling her that his father held a position of power but was off halfway around the world at a meeting and he was in charge of the empire while he was gone.

The woman had slept with his brother and drugged him. When Harbin had come around, he had realised his mistake and had rushed back to the village. It had been too late. Archangel, a hunter organisation, had already launched an attack on the pride. Cavanaugh had fought as hard as he could together with August and the other males, but while they had dealt with several of the hunters, they had lost many of their kin too.

His mother and sister included.

Harbin had returned shortly after the remaining hunters had fled. He had lost his mind on seeing their mother and younger sister laying in the snow, surrounded by stark crimson. Cavanaugh had tried to stop him, but he had gone after the hunters.

Harbin had returned several days later, naked and bloodied, his eyes as cold as ice.

Cavanaugh had done his best to console his brother, but to this day he wasn't sure whether his words had gotten through to Harbin at all. His brother had changed, all of the light and fire in him gone, leaving only darkness and ice behind.

The second their father had set foot in the village, he had announced Harbin's sentence. He had exiled him without even looking at him and had him ejected from the village without even giving him a chance to gather his things.

Cavanaugh had wanted to go after him, but their father had made it clear that if he attempted it, he would be banished too.

He had looked at Eloise then, seeing a woman he was falling in love with, one he couldn't live without, and had made the hard decision to stay where he was and let Harbin go.

Cavanaugh hadn't seen him since he had left the pride and all his attempts to track him down in the past five years had ended in nothing.

If Cavanaugh died as the alpha right now, the pride would pass to August.

"August should have done something," he muttered and ground his teeth. His cousin was younger than he was, but strong, more than able to rally the other males.

"He tried."

Those two words stopped him dead and he looked back over his shoulder at Eloise.

She closed her eyes, sucked down a sharp breath, and then opened them again. "August fought Stellan, but with his lackeys, Stellan was too strong for him."

"He should have convinced the other males to fight with him."

Pity filled her eyes. "The other males won't fight, Cavanaugh. Anyone who dared to raise his voice against Stellan was dealt with."

"He killed them?" The thought of his pride losing so many males shook him, but the way Eloise's golden-brown eyes shone with tears said that what had taken place was infinitely worse than he had imagined.

"He killed their females... and then he threatened to kill their young if they stepped out of line again."

Cavanaugh's knees weakened. No. He shook his head, not wanting to believe what she was saying, because in the end he was responsible for everything that had happened. His heart couldn't take it.

"I'm sorry." She placed her hand on his arm and squeezed it, lowering her gaze there. "This isn't your fault, Cavanaugh."

"It is." He placed his hand over hers and closed his eyes. "It is my fault. All of it. Everything that happened to you... everything that vile bastard did to the members of our pride... every death is blood on my hands, Eloise."

She stepped up to him and wrapped her arms around his shoulders, pulling him down against her. He settled his head on her shoulder, slid his arms around her waist, and held her, hating how weak he felt. He wanted to be at the village now, spilling Stellan's blood as retribution for the things he had done, but it would be suicide. He was in no fit state to fight, not against a male who had bested him before and had come close to killing him.

He had never been so glad that his animal instincts had forced him to survive, to escape with his life from a fight that should have claimed it.

Because he was going to make Stellan suffer for every life he had stolen, every punishment he had ordered and carried out, and every female he had taken against her will.

Cavanaugh was going to tear him to pieces.

"Cavanaugh?" Eloise murmured softly and stroked his hair, smoothing her fingers through it and smoothing out his feelings at the same time, bringing his anger down from a raging boil to a steady simmer in his veins. She pressed a kiss to his cheek and sighed against his skin, the warmth of her breath instantly giving way to the cold.

"I'm good." He settled his hands on her hips, pulled down a final deep breath to rein in his need to spill blood, and stepped back from her. He lifted his eyes to meet hers, finding them filled with warmth and concern. "I'm sorry about everything."

"There's no need to keep saying that." She brushed the backs of her fingers across his cheek and smiled.

"There is... there's every need for me to keep saying it... because no matter how many times I say it, it isn't enough. It won't be enough until I end this."

"I know." She lowered her gaze and her smile fell away.

He cursed her. He hadn't meant to bring up what would happen when they returned to the village, making her believe that he would take his place as alpha again, leaving her alone once more. What she had said to him about her mother came crashing back down on his shoulders, weighing heavily on his heart, and he sighed as he thought about it.

He should have been there for Eloise. She had been close to her mother, and so had he. He had always felt that she had approved of their match, and he had known she had disapproved when he had taken the position of alpha and had been unable to see Eloise. He had hoped to find her alive and well at the pride, because he had wanted to show her that he was trying to do the right thing.

Cavanaugh looked at Eloise, torn between asking the question burning on the tip of his tongue and remaining silent. He didn't want to hurt her, but he needed to know.

"Eloise," he started and then faltered when she looked up at him, right into his eyes. He exhaled hard and released her waist. "Your mother... did Stellan..."

He couldn't finish that question and the look in her eyes said that he didn't need to in order for her to understand.

She shook her head and relief beat through him, swift and soothing.

"It was natural causes," she said and he sent a silent thank you to the gods for granting him that small mercy.

He didn't know what he would have done if she had said that Stellan had killed her mother, but it would have torn his heart to shreds.

"I should've been there." He looked over his left shoulder, into the distance towards the village.

"She would have liked that." Eloise's soft words drew his gaze back to her. There was no anger in them, no hurt, not as there had been when she had told him that her mother had died. She reached out and took his hand, pressing her thumb into his palm, and stared at it. "She still loved you."

That didn't make him feel better.

"She went to her grave disappointed with me and believing I had left you alone in the world forever." He sighed and shook his head, and then twisted her hand in his and toyed with her fingers. Her black thermal gloves blended into his. "I've failed so many people."

"You haven't failed me." She placed her free hand against his face, tipped his head up and met his gaze. "You wanted to be free of a role you hated, and you seized the chance the gods gave to you. You didn't know what would happen. It wasn't your fault that Stellan turned on his own people."

"I was thinking only of myself." He huffed and stepped back, breaking contact between them. "I should have thought of the others. I was their alpha, dammit, and I should have acted like it. Instead I thought only of myself and what I wanted."

"No." She grabbed his hand again and held it tightly, her fingers crushing his together, and frowned up at him, her honey-coloured eyes flashing fire. "You didn't only think of yourself and what you wanted. You thought of me too... you thought of us... you thought of what we wanted."

Her voice trailed off into a whisper at the end, the strength fading from her eyes at the same time, and she released him and looked down into the valley, turning her profile to him.

Cavanaugh heaved a sigh.

Maybe he had been thinking of both of them, but they were only two out of many, and he still should have placed his pride before his own desires. He had been too quick to seize his chance to escape a life he hated and return to the one he loved.

The one where they were together.

The one he would have with her.

He needed to tell her that she was his mate and that he had no intention of reprising his role as alpha. He needed to tell her everything now, before they were back in the village.

"Eloise—"

A roar cut him off and he spun on his heel, looking along the path behind him, the one that led to the village. Nothing. Snow tumbled over the track. His gaze shot left and his heart froze in his chest before exploding into action.

A large male dressed in white winter gear skidded down the sloping side of the mountain towards him, disturbing the snow and sending it rolling down ahead of him. Two more men followed close behind him. A patrol team from the village.

"Eloise, run." He pushed her just as the first male reached them, sending her stumbling backwards along the track, towards the edge of the plateau. "Get down the mountain."

She shook her head and he cut her off with a snarl, flashing his fangs at her, commanding her to obey him. She shot him a wounded look and then turned and ran, her dark pack bouncing with each step.

The brunet male slammed into him, knocking him backwards and sending them both tumbling down the slope towards the valley below. Cavanaugh grappled with the male as they fell, struggling to land his blows and evade the ones the male threw at him as they rolled, bouncing off boulders beneath the snow. He struck one hard and grunted as the air whooshed out of his lungs and his head turned.

He was in no condition to fight, not against three males who were accustomed to the thinner air, but he needed to stop them, at least for a little while.

His gaze sought Eloise as the world twisted and spun around him, and he caught sight of her close to the end of the track where it dropped down onto the plateau. One of the males was going after her. The other was skidding down the slope, following Cavanaugh and his friend.

Cavanaugh hit the valley bottom hard. The male landed on top of him and Cavanaugh grunted as his weight pressed down on his stomach and lungs. He growled and shoved his palm up into the dark-haired male's face, snapping his head backwards. Before the male could recover, he landed a second blow, smashing his fist into his cheek and sending him falling sideways into the deep snow.

Cavanaugh scrambled onto his feet just as the second male barrelled into him, taking him down again. His pack pressed into his back, bending him at a painful angle beneath the male. He grabbed the blond's arm and pushed it upwards as he rolled, gaining the upper hand and pinning the male beneath him.

He grinned and punched the blond hard, one after the other, snapping his head right and then left. The scent of blood joined the metallic odour of snow as he slammed his fist into the male's nose.

Maybe he stood a chance after all.

The brunet grabbed Cavanaugh's hair as he swung another punch at the male beneath him and hauled him backwards, making him miss his target. He growled and reached over behind him, snagging the male's wrist, and went to throw him over his head.

Eloise shrieked.

Cavanaugh's head snapped towards her in time to see her crumple onto the snow.

He roared at the male who loomed behind her, his arm still outstretched from the blow he had delivered, and threw the one who stood behind him over his head, sending him crashing down on top of his companion.

Cavanaugh launched to his feet and ran as fast as he could through the snow, determined to reach Eloise. She wasn't moving. He growled through his emerging fangs and ran harder, his head spinning as his lungs burned and his heart laboured.

His left foot landed hard on the ground beneath him and his knee buckled, sending him face first into the snow. He snarled and struggled back onto his feet, forcing himself to keep going. He lumbered forwards, the world twirling around him.

"Eloise," he whispered and reached for her. He was close.

The male standing over her turned to face him. A thick rope dangled from his right fist.

Cavanaugh roared at the sight of it.

He wouldn't let the male lay his filthy hands on his female.

His Eloise.

He staggered forwards and swung a wild blow at the male, who easily dodged his clumsy attempt, and collapsed into the snow beside her. He breathed hard, staring at her pale face and the blood trickling down her left cheek from beneath her hat.

Eloise.

He reached for her.

Pain exploded across the back of his skull.

The world went black.

CHAPTER 13

Pain burned through Cavanaugh's body, fiercest in his head and in his arms. He tried to move them in front of him but they didn't budge. Awareness slowly dawned, understanding that his wrists were shackled behind him. The cold metal bit into his bare skin.

Icy wet froze his left side, from his shoulder down to his feet. They were bare too. The only item of clothing left on him was his trousers and the wetness of them said someone had removed the weatherproof layer, leaving him in only his light grey trousers. His enemy meant to keep him cold, draining the strength from him and making it hard for him to move, his muscles quick to tense and grow fatigued.

He breathed slowly, settling his heart and checking his condition. Based on the fact he could breathe easier and no longer felt weak from the thinner air, he had been out cold for a while, long enough for him to acclimatise to the altitude. Several hours, if not more. How long had he been at the village? He needed to know. The three men couldn't have carried both him and Eloise to the village before nightfall. It wasn't possible.

He focused his senses, bringing them slowly back online, using them to check out his surroundings without opening his eyes. A number of people surrounded him, some of their scents familiar. Eloise was there. He wanted to open his eyes and see her, but forced himself to wait. His captors weren't aware that he was conscious and he had to use that to his advantage.

He could smell the three who had attacked him and Eloise.

And he could smell Stellan.

He couldn't catch August's scent. Had Stellan done something to him to keep him away?

Cavanaugh suspected he was in the square in the middle of the village. If the metal ribs pressing into his side were anything to go by, he was caged as well as shackled. Not good.

He placed the three who had attacked him directly ahead of him with Stellan. Two more were there with them. The five lackeys that Eloise had told him about. The two he had fought were strong, but nothing compared with Stellan. Cavanaugh could easily deal with them now that he had acclimatised, even with the cold draining his strength and slowing him down.

He slowly manoeuvred onto his knees, grimacing as the metal shackles holding his wrists behind him settled on his lower back, chilling and burning his bare skin at the same time.

A murmur ran through the crowd.

Cavanaugh opened his eyes, pinning them straight on Stellan where he stood at the edge of the five-foot-high dark stone platform a short distance from him, blue sky and mountaintops as his backdrop. The position of the sun told Cavanaugh that it was late morning but didn't answer his question about how long he had been in the village.

The black-haired male's green eyes were on someone else.

He tracked Stellan's gaze and his stomach plummeted when he saw Eloise.

She lay slumped against a thick wooden post just metres from him in the centre of the square, a rope tightly tied around her wrists, pinning them above her head. She shivered constantly, her teeth chattering, her lips almost blue and her skin red raw as she rested in the compressed snow in only her underwear. Blood tracked down her cheek and smeared across her neck, forming a handprint. Someone had throttled her.

"You fucking bastard." Cavanaugh launched himself at the bars of his cramped six-foot-square cage, slamming his shoulder into the metal rods with such force that the entire cage shifted forward several inches.

His blood boiled as he attacked the thick bars, kicking them, each blow sending sharp stabbing pain up his leg bones. He turned around to grasp two bars in his hands and braced his bare feet against the bottom of the cage as he heaved forwards, trying to break them.

Stellan chuckled.

Cavanaugh turned on him with a roar that shook the mountains, echoing around them for long after he had finished. He breathed hard, his gaze constantly leaping between Stellan and Eloise.

He needed to escape the damned cage and reach her. His kind could withstand extreme cold, but not for long, and definitely not when they were naked and kneeling in the snow.

"Eloise." He pressed his forehead against the bars closest to her and kneeled, willing her to hear him. "Eloise."

She moaned and a frown flickered on her brow.

"Come on, Eloise, Baby," he murmured, his heart pounding against his ribs. "Let me see you're okay."

She grimaced and tried to lift her head, the tangled threads of her damp dark hair falling away from her face as she raised it. Her lips parted, reopening the cut that dashed across her lower one. Her eyes opened and he cursed as they met his. They were haunted again, no longer bright and shining as they had been throughout their journey.

"Let her go," he snapped at Stellan. "She hasn't done anything. Let her go."

Stellan didn't move. His cold green eyes remained impassive.

"Fuck you." Cavanaugh bared his fangs at the male and then turned on the people gathered around the square, forming a circle.

Doing nothing but stare at her.

"Help her." He pinned every single one who dared to look at him with a glare. "Do something. She'll die if you don't, dammit. She risked her life to bring me back for your sakes and you do nothing when she needs you?"

Everyone looked away, lowering their gazes to the snow, and some even turned around, looking as if they might leave and head back to one of the many two-storey buildings that formed the village around the square.

How many times had he and Eloise walked through this square together, laughing in the sunshine, admiring the beauty of the village and the mountains that protected it from the outside world?

The elaborate buildings, with their pale stone ground floor and their upper floor with its white panels surrounded by dark carved wood, and topped with a low angled roof were no longer beautiful to him. The mountains that rose beyond them were no longer stunning. The whole place felt cold and desolate, one that had lost its charm for him years ago. It had faded more every day that he'd had to remain apart from Eloise, watching her from a distance.

There was no beauty in this world without her at his side.

Without her smile.

Without her laughter.

Without the way she would look at him with a trace of shyness mixed with affection in her honey-coloured eyes.

Cavanaugh roared and attacked the cage again, rattling it and tearing a few gasps from the gathered.

"Do something!" He wedged his right shoulder against the bars of his cage and breathed hard, staring at his kin, silently imploring them to do as he asked because he had never asked them to do anything before now, and now he was asking them to save his Eloise. "Please."

A few exchanged glances and then quickly looked away from him when Stellan growled. They were scared, he could understand that after everything they had been through, but there were many of them and only a few who stood with Stellan. If he could rally them, give them the courage to rise up against Stellan, they could win without his help.

"I'm begging you," he whispered and looked at Eloise, aching with a need to pull her into his arms and hold her as she stared blankly at him through dull lifeless eyes. "Save her. You don't need an alpha to lead you... together you're strong... you can help her."

He looked back at them. A quiet murmur ran through the crowd, more of them swapping glances now, and he knew the tide was turning. He could inspire them to take up arms and fight for their pride.

"I should have silenced you when I met my men at the edge of the village this morning and they were dragging your worthless unconscious body through the snow, together with your bitch." Stellan dropped down from the platform and strode towards the cage, the snow crunching beneath his thick leather boots. He was stark black against pure white as he stood before Cavanaugh, his top lip curling to reveal a short fang. "I wanted to make an example of you though. You'll die today, here, in front of all these people... and when they see their strongest male die like every other male who tried to stand against me... they'll obey my every command without question, forever."

Cavanaugh bit back the growl that rumbled up his throat.

He had been wrong. His kin hadn't gathered out of choice. They had been forced to come and witness his execution.

Stellan stepped back and the blond and brunet males who had fought Cavanaugh leaped off the platform, landing close to him. They strode past their alpha, the blond taking a key from him, and stopped at the door of Cavanaugh's cage.

They were going to release him.

The blond unlocked the door of the cage and the dark-haired one reached in, grabbed Cavanaugh by his hair and pulled him out, shoving him down onto his knees on the snow in front of Stellan. They stood sentinel over him and he breathed slowly, calming himself. As much as he wanted to throw himself at Stellan and bite the bastard, he had to be patient.

He couldn't risk being knocked unconscious again. He was stronger now that he had acclimatised but he was still at a disadvantage with his hands bound behind his back. When the moment came, he would launch his attack. He just had to wait and then he would use the ace he had up his sleeve.

Stellan had overlooked something critical and Cavanaugh was more than happy to exploit it in order to put the bastard down.

Out of the corner of his right eye, Cavanaugh spotted August among the people gathered on that side of the square. The black skullcap he wore hid his wild red hair, but Cavanaugh would recognise his silver eyes anywhere. He stood at the back of the group, another male beside him. Instinct told Cavanaugh that his cousin would fight the moment he made his move, joining him in his battle against Stellan.

Cavanaugh could only hope everyone else would follow his lead.

He hoped that what he was about to do would inspire them to rise up against Stellan too.

Stellan drew a short silver blade from a sheath at his waist.

He took a step towards Cavanaugh.

Cavanaugh unleashed every drop of the fury he had been storing up throughout the journey, every ounce of the rage he felt as he looked at his mate, seeing her beaten and on the verge of freezing to death. It poured through his muscles and veins like acid, seared his bones and set him on fire.

He roared as he pulled his wrists apart, his shoulders and chest straining as he fought against the metal.

The steel links between the two thick cuffs shattered and he fell forwards with the sudden release of his wrists, pressing his hands into the snow.

Stellan's green eyes shot wide and he unleashed his own roar as he recovered from the shock of seeing Cavanaugh break solid metal with only his natural strength.

Cavanaugh grinned, revealing his fangs, and kicked off, launching himself at Stellan. Breaking the chain between the shackles had been the easy part, his ace that he had known would catch Stellan off guard, leaving him open to attack. The temperature was well below zero degrees centigrade, the cold significantly weakening the thin metal and making it brittle.

What came next was the hard part.

Stellan swung a wild blow with his sword and Cavanaugh skidded beneath it, sliding across the packed snow. He kicked out with his right leg as he reached the black-haired male, catching him in the back of his left knee and sending him crashing onto the ground. He slid past Stellan, stopping only when his bare feet hit the stone platform. He turned on his front and kicked off, propelling himself forwards, towards Stellan.

The male raised his hand in a command. The three males who had remained on the platform leaped down off it just as Cavanaugh connected hard with Stellan's back, slamming him face first onto the icy ground. The three males ran at Cavanaugh and he rolled, evading the blow he felt coming. The male barely managed to avoid striking Stellan and skidded on the snow, losing his footing.

Before the other two could attempt to attack him, August and his comrade were there, taking them on.

As soon as the others saw August fighting, the younger males among them broke out from the crowd and launched an attack on the brunet and blond males who were coming to aid Stellan.

Cavanaugh looked across to check on Eloise and heat swept through him, burning away his fear, as he saw a group of young females leaping in to save her.

Now he could give Stellan his undivided attention.

The black-haired male was back on his feet, his green eyes darkening dangerously as he turned on Cavanaugh.

Cavanaugh bared his fangs on a snarl and rushed towards him. Stellan had lost his only advantage. The blade. It lay near the cage in the churned up snow. If Cavanaugh could get his hands on it, he could end this fight before anyone was hurt. Stellan's lackeys were the sort of men who would quickly surrender if they saw their leader fall.

Stellan met him halfway, throwing a hard left hook. Cavanaugh dodged it but not the swift uppercut that followed. It connected with his jaw, snapping his head upwards, and he grunted as his skull ached from the force of the blow. He dropped his head back down and swung his right fist, following it with a low left blow. As predicted, Stellan shifted to his right to dodge Cavanaugh's first punch, placing himself directly in the path of his second.

Cavanaugh growled as he slammed his left fist up into Stellan's kidney, lifting the male inches off the ground with the hard blow. Stellan grunted and Cavanaugh clasped his hands together and swung them upwards in a fast arc as Stellan stumbled backwards. The manacles around Cavanaugh's wrists smashed into the side of Stellan's head and the scent of blood filled the air as the male went down hard. The shackle around Cavanaugh's right wrist fractured and he yanked it off as he backed away from Stellan, gaining some space.

One more shackle and then he could shift. Right now, the tight metal was stopping him. If he shifted, he would injure his front leg, placing himself at a disadvantage.

Stellan launched at him and Cavanaugh grunted as the male barrelled into him, his shoulder punching hard into his stomach and knocking the wind from him. He grappled with the male's shoulders and brought his knee up, slamming it into Stellan's chest. The male gasped but didn't release him. Cavanaugh linked his hands again, raised them above his head as he skidded backwards with Stellan driving him, and brought them down in a swift arc, using every drop of strength available to him.

His fists struck hard in the centre of Stellan's back, driving the male downwards. Stellan lost his grip and Cavanaugh didn't hesitate. He brought his knee up again, smashing it into Stellan's face. The scent of blood grew stronger and Stellan shoved away from him, moving to a distance, his hand covering his face. Blood dripped from his chin and onto the white snow.

Cavanaugh breathed hard. Something flashed in Stellan's eyes.

Cavanaugh's own eyes widened as he sensed someone behind him and began to turn. The blond male was too fast, looping his arms under Cavanaugh's from behind before he could shift away from him and bringing them over his shoulders. The male locked his hands behind Cavanaugh's head and he snarled as he fought the blond's hold on him.

Stellan looked towards the blade.

The blond chuckled.

August tossed Cavanaugh a worried look as he fought the dark-haired male.

His cousin didn't need to worry.

He had this.

Cavanaugh roared as he tipped forwards, hurling the male over his head and sending him crashing into the snow. The second the male released him, he brought his right fist down hard, smashing it into his face. The blond grunted and blood spewed from his nose. Stellan growled and Cavanaugh sensed his approach.

He turned swiftly and brought his leg up, blocking the kick Stellan had launched at him, their shins connecting hard and sending pain blazing up his bones. He growled, drew his leg back and kicked again, sending his foot flying at Stellan's hip. It struck the dip of his waist and Cavanaugh grunted as he forced himself to follow through, sending Stellan flying across the square.

Stellan struck the cage, knocking it back several feet, and fell onto the snow where it had been.

Right next to the sword.

Not exactly what Cavanaugh had planned.

He kicked off, his gaze locked on the blade and his heart pounding. He had to reach it before Stellan regained his senses and realised how close to victory he was.

Cavanaugh's bare foot slipped on the icy ground and he slammed face-first into it, grunting as his lungs took the brunt of the impact.

Stellan was on his feet by the time Cavanaugh recovered, skidding around as he tried to stand, and had the blade in his hand before Cavanaugh could reach him. The black-haired male turned on him with a vicious smile and Cavanaugh backed off, scanning the fight for something he could use as a weapon.

He needed something, or he needed a way of distracting Stellan long enough that he could reach him and get the weapon off him.

August roared.

Cavanaugh's gaze swung towards where he had last seen him, spotting him just as he shifted, becoming a huge snow leopard. August growled and sprang, leaping high in the air and sailing towards Stellan.

Stellan turned towards him.

Cavanaugh cursed August for making such a reckless move and raced towards Stellan, his heart thundering as he tried to close the distance between them before Stellan could cut his cousin down.

Stellan swung the blade, cutting through the air with it, directly where August's chest would be any second now. Cavanaugh roared as he hurled himself at Stellan. Not quick enough. He slammed into Stellan, knocking him down, but not before the tip of the blade sliced across August's right shoulder.

Cavanaugh landed hard on top of Stellan. The blade skidded away from both of them, towards the pole where Eloise had been tied up. August crashed to the ground, whimpering as he transformed back, the pain of his injury forcing him to shift.

The male August had been with was beside him in an instant, covering him as he fought both the blond and another male from Stellan's side.

Cavanaugh needed to help him.

He grabbed Stellan's head and slammed it hard against the frozen ground, hoping it was enough to keep him down for a few seconds while he checked on his cousin.

He shoved off Stellan and raced through the fray to August, ducking beneath blows as Stellan's men tried to stop him. When he reached August, he kneeled and checked him over. The cut across his shoulder was deep, but not life threatening. He breathed a sigh of relief when August opened his silver eyes, staring up at him.

"Idiot," Cavanaugh muttered and helped him onto his feet. He turned to his comrade, who was still fending off the two men, his broad back to Cavanaugh. "Get him to safety."

"No. I can still fight."

Cavanaugh hadn't wanted to hear those words leaving August's lips. He turned a frown on his cousin and the red-haired male didn't back down. He had grown stronger in the time they had been apart, and Cavanaugh was glad to see it. August had grown into a powerful male, and the pride would need him now more than ever.

"Fine. But if you get yourself killed, it's your own damned fault." Cavanaugh slapped a hand down on August's good shoulder and then turned and formed an allied front with him, facing off against three of the males from Stellan's group. The other two lay out cold on the snow.

Three on three sounded good to him, but he had a date with another male.

"Can you handle this?" he said to August and saw him nod out of the corner of his eye. "Be careful."

Cavanaugh didn't wait for him to respond before throwing himself at the blond male directly in front of him. He ducked beneath the male's first blow, leaped back to avoid the second, and sprang forwards to deliver one of his own, landing it hard on the male's jaw and snapping his head to his right. The male lost his footing and almost fell. Cavanaugh dodged past him, leaving his cousin to deal with him, and went after Stellan.

He spotted the black-haired bastard gunning for the sword again.

Cavanaugh growled and brought his right fist down hard on the shackle that remained around his left wrist, striking it. It wouldn't budge. He needed to get it off. He looked at the stone platform off to his right and grinned as he changed direction, heading towards it.

The second he was within reach, he gritted his teeth against the pain that was coming and swung his wrist down onto the dark grey stone. The shackle shattered and he flinched away, closing his eyes as pieces of metal sprayed everywhere.

Cavanaugh roared.

Stellan stopped looking for the sword and swung to face him.

The people between them got Cavanaugh's message loud and clear too and moved out of the line of fire. Space formed between him and Stellan.

Stellan's green eyes flashed and he reached over his head, grasping the back of his black jumper.

He wouldn't be quick enough.

Cavanaugh roared again as the transformation came over him, his limbs quick to shift beneath his skin as he kicked off, launching himself towards Stellan as the male tossed his jumper and fumbled with his shirt.

Silver fur swept over Cavanaugh's body. His tail sprouted from the base of his spine as he came free of his trousers and his face morphed, his ears shifting upwards and rounding, and his eyes growing larger. The world brightened. The smells grew clearer. The air tasted crisper.

He opened his jaws as he completed his transformation and unleashed a longer roar as his paws pounded against the snow, their width and his claws giving him purchase on the slippery surface. He sprang at Stellan just as the male managed to get his top off. His green eyes shot wide and Cavanaugh snarled as his front paws struck the male's chest, the force of his blow knocking him backwards. Stellan skidded on the ground and fell.

Cavanaugh's back paws struck Stellan's legs and he landed on top of him on the snow. Before Stellan could even grunt from the impact, Cavanaugh struck. He angled his head, clamped his jaws down on the male's throat, and growled as blood flooded his mouth.

Stellan bellowed in agony and lifted his hand, silver glinting in it and catching Cavanaugh's attention.

The sword.

It zoomed towards him, aimed directly for his neck.

Cavanaugh hadn't wanted to resort to such vile methods of dispatching his foe, but Stellan gave him no choice.

He clamped down harder with his jaws and pulled his head back, ripping Stellan's throat out.

The blade slowed as Stellan gurgled, blood pumping from the vicious wound and spilling across the white snow, spreading outwards from beneath him.

Cavanaugh snarled as Stellan's arm dropped and the silver sword grazed him, slicing down his left shoulder. He spat out the contents of his mouth onto Stellan's still chest and backed off, huffing as he breathed hard. The smell of his own blood joined that of his enemy.

The world around him stilled, falling silent as all eyes swung his way.

He closed his eyes and focused, shifting back into his human form. Blood spilled from the wound on his shoulder as his bones snapped back into place and his fur swept down his body, revealing pink skin. He grunted and pressed a hand over the long gash, stemming the flow of blood down his chest, and kneeled in the snow, breathing hard.

Someone placed a blanket around his shoulders.

Others drew closer, staring at Stellan where he lay with his green gaze fixed sightlessly on the sky, surrounded by a stark red pool of blood.

Cavanaugh looked away from him, seeking the only person he needed to see right now, the one who had given him the strength to fight.

His eyes drifted over all the people and then beyond them, down the alleys between the buildings. He spotted what he needed to see there, two females carrying her up the set of wooden steps of her small two-storey home near the back of the village.

"Cavanaugh?" August crouched beside him and he spared his cousin a glance before rising onto his feet, wrapping the blanket around him and holding it with one hand, still clutching his shoulder with the other.

He drifted through the village, unaware of everyone as they tried to speak with him and his cousin as he tried to get his attention. The chatter of his kin fell away as his focus narrowed to one person.

Eloise.

When he reached her small home, the two females were leaving. They bowed their heads but he paid them no heed. He mounted the wooden steps and entered her home, following his senses through the cramped open living area to the stairs to the upper floor against the back wall. He slowly ascended them and looked across to his right as the next floor and the only other room in the house came into view. She lay swathed in colourful quilts on her small bed that stood directly in front of the bend at the top of the stairs, against the left wall of the room.

He reached the top of the stairs and glanced at the window to the right of the bed, looking out of it at the other buildings and the view back to the square. His kin and his village, all of it meant nothing to him right now. They could take care of themselves, because he needed to be here, taking care of Eloise.

He would take care of the female he loved.

He kneeled beside the head of the bed near the window, his back to the fireplace as he faced her, and released his blanket, letting it fall away from his body as he devoted all of his focus to her. He stroked her tangled wet hair from her cold brow.

His beautiful female.

She was the only one in the world for him, and she would become his mate.

He swallowed in an attempt to settle his nerves as they rose again, a reminder that so much had happened in the ten years they had been forced apart from each other, and much of what had happened had been his fault.

All he could do now was nurse her back to health and then speak from his heart, confessing everything, and hope that she would listen.

All he could do was hope that when all was said and done, she would put him out of his misery.

She would consent to being his mate.

He had defeated Stellan and set his pride free, but deep in his heart he knew his biggest fight was yet to come.

If he could win this one, he could win the forever he wanted with her.

CHAPTER 14

Eloise woke to the distant sound of merriment. It drifted through the walls of her home. A celebration. Her heart didn't lift at that thought. It dropped into her stomach and she had to fight to pull it back up from the pit of despair.

She slowly opened her eyes and frowned at her room. A fire burned in the grate off to her left, spreading warmth over her, and she stared at it as she gathered her strength. She touched the bandages around her wrists beneath the thick layers of covers. Someone had taken care of her. Her memory was patchy. She recalled being stripped and bound. She remembered seeing Cavanaugh in a cage and him calling her name. She knew he had fought.

She wasn't sure what the outcome of that fight had been.

Her memories grew blurry, a mishmash of being cut free, seeing her home, and then the faintest sense that someone had placed her into a hot bath and had taken care of her.

The last part must have been one of the females who had cut her free from the post and had pulled her away from the battle.

Eloise pushed the covers back, her muscles aching with the strain. She cursed how weak she felt and fought it, unwilling to let it get the better of her. She was stronger than this. She had to see what had happened.

She swung her legs over the edge of the bed, pressed her hands into the mattress, and slowly pushed onto her feet. Her knees threatened to buckle but held firm when she locked them. She used the furniture in her room to move around it to the wardrobe and opened the wooden cupboard. She took out her tan thick thermal trousers and a white thermal top, and slowly put them on, gaining balance and strength with each second she managed to remain on her feet. She followed them with a pair of wool socks and her boots, and then put on her white woollen jumper.

The stairs down to the ground level proved more of a problem than moving around her small bedroom and she almost fell at one point, saving herself by clutching the wooden bannister. She huffed, gave herself a moment to recover, and then continued, pushing past her fatigue. She needed to reach the centre of the village.

She had to see what was happening.

She carefully walked across the ground floor, slowly manoeuvring around her couch and armchair, and opened the wooden door. The cold hit her hard despite all her layers and she shivered, wishing she still had the gloves and hat that Cavanaugh had given her.

Cavanaugh.

Her heart fell again at just the sound of his name.

Her eyes sought the source of the noise in the village.

A huge bonfire blazed in the centre of the square ahead of her, partially hidden by the other buildings between her and it.

She closed her eyes and clung to the wooden doorframe for support as her knees weakened again. It was a celebration.

Cavanaugh had won.

Tears burned the backs of her eyes.

He was their alpha again.

Eloise pulled down a deep breath, hoping it would steady her. Her heart told her to go back inside, lock the door, and return to her bed. She didn't need to see this. She didn't need to hear the joy of the village.

She shook her head and growled through her clenched teeth. She was stronger than this. She had to see him, even though she knew that it would only hurt her. She needed to see that he was alright, and then she would come back and do as her heart wanted, sealing herself away from the world for a while.

Eloise trudged down the wooden steps to the snow and slowly wandered towards the celebration. All of the pride were there, talking and laughing as they surrounded the fire. It burned brightly, chasing back the dark of night. She looked up at the thick clouds that obscured the stars.

More snow was coming.

She could smell it in the crisp air.

She tried to busy her mind with everything she would need to do to prepare for the storm, but it kept slipping back to thoughts of Cavanaugh as she drew closer to the rowdy celebration. She approached from the main avenue between the houses, directly opposite the large stone platform on the other side of the square.

Cavanaugh stood there, dressed in dark winter clothing that hugged his tall, broad figure, his silver-white hair stark against the blackness beyond him, and the firelight twinkling in his eyes as he laughed with someone.

August.

His cousin stood beside him, looking like a fire god with his vivid red hair and his pure silver eyes. The male raised a steaming mug and Cavanaugh did the same, knocking them together. The local brew. It had always been too strong for her.

Cavanaugh had laughed his backside off the one time she had tried it and had fallen drunk almost instantly, and then he had taken care of her.

The smile that had been blooming on her lips died as she saw the females around the base of the platform, and some of the ones on the platform, were looking at Cavanaugh.

Her heart fractured, as fragile as ice in her chest.

Eloise clenched her fists and forced herself to look at the pride, at how happy they were now, freed from Stellan's rule. She was glad they were safe.

But it hurt too.

She felt as if she had just destroyed all of her hope and had sacrificed her one chance of being with Cavanaugh.

The celebration was about more than the defeat of a tyrant. It was a celebration of Cavanaugh becoming their alpha.

The same celebration she had been forced to endure a decade ago.

It had broken her heart back then, just as it broke her heart now.

Eloise sniffed back the tears that tried to fill her eyes and turned away from the celebration.

"Eloise," Cavanaugh called, his deep voice unmistakable as it rose above the noise, cutting at her with its warmth. She couldn't look back at him. She couldn't bear to see how he would be smiling, as if nothing was wrong. As if he felt no pain in this moment, only happiness. "You're up... I'm glad to see it. Where are you going?"

She felt the eyes of everyone coming to rest on her and cursed him for singling her out when she had only wanted to quietly slink back into the darkness.

The storm wouldn't hit for a day.

She had time to slip away and be far from this place that only brought her pain before it reached them.

"Eloise." His tone held a sharper note, one that demanded she look at him and answer his question.

She couldn't deny him. He was her pride's alpha after all.

She turned back to him and her breath hitched in her throat as she found him standing near the edge of the platform across the square, bathed in firelight. Gods, he was so handsome. The sight of him only increased the pain burning inside her, a terrible reminder of what she had sacrificed for the sake of her pride.

She bowed her head, unable to look at him any longer. "Away."

"Away?"

She nodded.

"Away where?"

Eloise clutched her hands in front of her hips and considered what she was about to say. She couldn't tell him the truth, but she wouldn't lie to him either.

"Anywhere but here," she said.

His tone hardened. "Why?"

She frowned, screwing her eyes shut. She didn't want to do this in front of everyone, but she had to abide by pride rules and answer him.

Eloise sucked down another sharp breath of cold air that cleared her lungs and her mind, and found the strength to lift her head and look straight at him. "I cannot remain here."

Cavanaugh's face darkened, the silver slashes of his eyebrows dropping low above his grey eyes. "Why not?"

She wanted to look away, almost gave in to that need, but managed to keep looking at him. "Because... I can't bear it."

He moved right to the edge of the stone platform and the crowd between them parted, leaving her feeling as if there was only her and Cavanaugh.

"You can't bear it?" He frowned at her, a confused edge to his gaze. "You have no reason to leave when you'll no longer be in danger of being forced into a harem."

She cursed him for seeing through her words to the truth beneath, that she wanted to leave this place entirely and never come back, and she cursed him for mentioning the harem. It made her look at the females surrounding him, staring at him with a mixture of adoration and surprise. Females of status. Women he would be expected to bed now that he was their alpha again.

Eloise's heart caught fire.

She took a hard step forwards, towards him, clenched her trembling fists at her side, and stared into his eyes. "I refuse to stay. I need to leave."

Cavanaugh shook his head. "I refuse to let you leave."

She stumbled back a step, her eyebrows furrowing as she searched his gaze, seeing that he meant what he had said. Shock rolled through her, anger that he would do such a thing to her following in its wake.

Eloise scowled at him and snapped, "Why?"

A collective gasp ran through those gathered around her. They murmured, no doubt speaking about her and what she had just done. She caught one person calling her disrespectful.

Cavanaugh smiled, as if her audacity had amused rather than angered him. Or maybe he liked that she had spoken out to him, treating him in the same manner as she had when they were younger, before he had become an alpha.

He set his mug down beside his boots and straightened, pinning his grey gaze back on her. "Why? You brought me back here, and now you're leaving. I'm the one who should be asking why."

Eloise almost lowered her eyes and then resolutely said, "There's no reason for me to remain. I left this place to bring you back for the sake of our pride. I've done that, and now I'm going to leave."

He didn't look as if he was going to listen to a word she had to say about what she wanted. "You have every reason to remain. This is your home."

"I'm still leaving." She ignored how everyone murmured again, casting scowls in her direction.

They couldn't stop her and neither could Cavanaugh. She had made up her mind.

"I cannot let you do that." He frowned at her, his expression darkening again. "You belong here."

Eloise took another step closer and stared at him, her anger burning in her veins and mixing with her pain, forming an explosive and dangerous combination that threatened to have her forgetting everything about pride rules and politics, and giving him a piece of her mind.

She barely bit back the growl that wanted to rumble up her throat and exhaled hard, trying to expel her fury so she could speak reasonably with him and make him listen to her.

If he felt anything for her, if what they had shared meant anything to him, he would listen and he would let her do what she felt was right for her.

He would spare her the pain that staying would only cause her.

She whispered, "Let me leave."

His eyebrows furrowed, his eyes leaping between hers, and she feared he would tell her no again.

He lifted his right hand towards her. "There are tears in your eyes."

She lowered her head and dashed them away, cursing herself for not realising and letting him see them and how much this was hurting her.

"You really don't want to stay here with me?" he husked and she lifted her gaze back to his and shook her head.

She swore he looked wounded in the instant before he smiled.

"What if I asked you to stay?" he said.

It wouldn't change anything. She wished that it would, but it wouldn't, and she didn't want to live that way again, hurting every time she saw him.

She closed her eyes, drew on her strength, and looked at him again, hoping he would see in her eyes everything she felt in her heart. There was only one way to make him let her go, and that was to say things straight and make her feelings clear. It would hurt like hell, and it might hurt him too, but it was better than staying and enduring years of hurt. She would take a swift stab straight through her heart over a long drawn out torture.

"No. I can't bear it. I couldn't back then and I can't now. I'm not strong enough. Please, Cavanaugh, let me leave."

His expression didn't shift. It remained impassive. "I cannot."

"Why not?" she barked, her voice echoing around the dark mountains.

He didn't answer her.

Tears filled her eyes and she tried to hold them back, but she no longer had the strength, not when a terrible realisation went through her.

He would force her to stay. He would force her to see him with other women, never with her. She clutched her chest, tugging her white jumper into her fist.

"I cannot be here, Cavanaugh. Please don't make me stay. Please don't make me see you again… with others." Her eyes searched his, a wildness consuming her, driven by panic and overwhelming pain.

"Others?" Confusion flickered on his handsome face.

Eloise closed her eyes and swallowed hard. "I understand. I know my place."

"I don't think you do." The hardness in his deep voice made her look at him.

He leaped down from the platform and strode towards her, the snow crunching beneath his boots. She backed off a step, sure he meant to put her in her place.

His right hand lifted.

His face softened and surprise claimed her when he carefully wiped her tears away with the pads of his thumbs and then cupped her cheeks, tilting her head up. Her eyes met his.

"I cannot let you leave," he whispered.

Eloise closed her eyes and leaned into his touch, trembling as his warmth seeped into her and his scent curled around her, soothing her pain.

"I cannot let you leave without me."

Her eyes shot open, leaping up to his.

He smiled and it hit her hard, knocking the breath from her. "There are no others, Eloise, and there never have been. There has only been you."

Her eyes widened.

His smile followed suit, curving wider, lighting up his eyes. "Whatever you think you saw, it never happened. There is only one female for me… there is only one I have ever craved… and only one who gave me the strength to do what I wanted. *You.*"

She opened her mouth to speak but he shook his head, silencing her.

"I left the pride because I couldn't have you, Eloise. I left because I wanted you and I hated the damned rules that meant I could never have you."

She stared at him, reeling and struggling to take it all in. He had told her back in the cave that she had been the reason he had left, but she hadn't realised the true depth of what he had been trying to tell her.

She knew it now.

It beat within her, a drumming in her blood. It flowed through her veins and gave her strength and courage as everything she had felt during the course of her entire life suddenly made sense.

"You don't know your place," Cavanaugh whispered, earnest and beautiful as he looked down into her eyes, his grey ones soft and filled with affection. "Because you clearly haven't realised that your place is with me. Nothing can keep me from you, can't you see that? Nothing. I left because I wanted you and nothing else. I wanted the only thing that could make me happy... make me strong... and make me feel like the king of these mountains."

He lowered his head towards hers, narrowing her focus down to only him.

"I wanted my mate."

Shivers ran down her arms and her thighs, spreading over her scalp as a smile burst onto her lips and all of her fears and her pain fell away.

"I know you feel it too now," he murmured and stroked her cheeks with his thumbs, his gaze searching hers. "Deep inside you, you know that we were made for each other. We were destined to be mates."

She nodded and he smiled at her, a light filling his eyes that warmed her. Her Cavanaugh. She had thought she had lost him again, but he was right here in front of her, holding her and speaking his heart to her.

Her mate.

"When did you realise?" she said, needing to know because it had only just dawned on her. She had only just pieced together everything and made the discovery that he had clearly been aware of for much longer.

He smoothed his thumbs over her cheeks again. "The night before my father died, when we—"

Eloise clapped a hand over his mouth and blushed as he mumbled the rest into her palm. She didn't need him telling the entire pride about their personal affairs and how they had been each other's first, and only.

Cavanaugh released her left cheek, curled his fingers around her wrist and drew her hand away from his mouth. He pressed a kiss to her knuckles, his eyes locked on hers.

"But I fell in love with you before that."

Those words and the boyish look in his eyes stole her heart all over again. She could only smile at him as she stared into his eyes, letting everything crash over her and sweep her away.

"You were in love with me too, weren't you?" he husked and pressed another kiss to her fingers.

Eloise turned her hand, capturing his, and brought it down to her lips.

She pressed a kiss to his palm. "I'm still in love with you."

She could feel his relief as it went through him, but that same emotion didn't run through her.

He loved her, and she loved him, but it was a bittersweet moment because she knew it couldn't be.

The rules he had spoken of still kept them apart, and now it would hurt her more than ever, because now she knew how much it was going to hurt him too.

She went to release his hand but he caught hold of her wrist, stopping her from pulling away.

"You can leave," he said and her heart fell before he lifted it up again. "But you're leaving with me."

Eloise shook her head. Had he lost his mind?

"You can't leave," she snapped and looked around them at everyone. "The pride... you're the alpha."

Cavanaugh smoothed his palm across her cheek and slowly brought her eyes back to his. He smiled down into them.

"I'm not."

"You what?" She stared deep into his eyes, convinced he really had lost his mind or someone had hit him very hard on the head.

His smile widened and he looked up at the sky. "I lost the right to being the alpha. All I did was kill an alpha and free up a spot for a new one."

She shook her head, sure the world had suddenly taken a strange turn, and looked up at the sky, following his gaze. The moon peeked through a break in the clouds.

It had passed its apex.

It was already waning. No longer full.

Eloise dropped her gaze to him. "But I counted the days..."

His smile gained a mischievous edge. "You might have lost one... in the cave... when you were unconscious."

"What?" Eloise couldn't believe it. She had been out cold for more than a day and he hadn't told her. He had known she was counting the days. He hadn't told her that she had lost one.

She could only stare at him as that sank in, sending her head spinning and her heart soaring.

He had set foot in the village after the moon had become full.

He wasn't their alpha.

Her blood chilled a degree.

But he could be.

"You defeated our alpha. You challenged him and you won. Will you accept the right of the victor?" Her heart raced as she waited for him to put her out of her misery, a trickle of fear running through her even when she knew deep in her heart that he didn't want to be their alpha.

"No." He placed his hands on her waist, slowly drawing her towards him. "I never wanted that position. I may have eliminated a threat to our pride, but the rules I can't abide still exist. If I had taken the role of alpha again, my title would have still been a barrier between us."

He had already let it pass to another. He had given the pride to August.

Cavanaugh drew her closer still, until she could feel his heat and she itched to step into his embrace.

"I never had any intention of becoming the pride's alpha again, Eloise." His eyes darted between hers and his mischievous smile returned, telling her that he would have found a way to delay her if she hadn't knocked herself unconscious. He could have distracted her for days in that cave and she wouldn't have cared, because it had felt too good to be with him. "I had no intention of letting anything come between us again. I left because I wanted you as my mate, not because Stellan defeated me. I messed up… I should have done some things differently… but all I could think about was passing five years away from the pride so I could be free to be with you. I am free to be with you… and all I want is forever with you."

She wanted that so much and she knew that he did too. He had made a life for himself in London, at the nightclub, and perhaps they could make a life there together. She wanted that.

"Will you have me?" he whispered and she almost laughed at how nervous he looked and the way his hands trembled against her.

As if she would turn down the only thing she had ever wanted.

Cavanaugh as hers.

She stepped into him, wrapped her arms around his neck, and drew him down for a soft kiss.

She whispered against his lips.

"I've wanted forever with you for longer than I can remember."

He gathered her into his arms and kissed her hard, and she blushed as a cheer went up, reminding her that they weren't alone.

She didn't care.

All she cared about was the male in her arms, holding her pinned against his body, his lips searing hers with a kiss that melted her heart.

Her Cavanaugh.

Her fated mate.

Everything she had ever wanted.

CHAPTER 15

Cavanaugh sat at the top of the wooden steps outside Eloise's house, his back against the door and his gaze fixed on the distant square and the celebration happening there. August had been happy to take the title of alpha, lifting the weight from Cavanaugh's shoulders. His cousin had proven himself a strong male and he was happy leaving the pride in his hands.

Eloise sighed and leaned back against him. She sat wedged between his thighs, her arms resting over his as they circled her waist. He held her gently even though she had recovered from her injuries. She had been surprised when he had told her that he had been the one to take care of her and had rewarded him with an achingly tender kiss when he had promised he would always take care of her. It had been a struggle to deny his urge to draw her into his arms and deepen that kiss, taking things further. He had wanted to make love to her and claim her as his mate.

He had been fighting that need since the night she had come to the bonfire and he had told her that she was his fated female.

She settled her head on his shoulder and hummed along with the song the pride were singing, a traditional folk one that welcomed the new alpha.

He tightened his hold on her, thinking back ten years to when he had endured hearing that song and had hated every second of it. He had despised the week-long celebration of his attaining the title of alpha. It had made him keenly feel how everything he cared about had been ruthlessly stripped away from him as each traditional part of the celebration slowly shoved him into a role he had never wanted.

Eloise patted his arm, as if she was aware of his thoughts. He took the comfort she offered, holding her closer to him and reassuring himself that his ten long years of misery were over now. Everything he had wanted was back in his arms.

Back within his reach.

He dropped a kiss on her shoulder, her thick warm jumper soft against his lips, and then pressed a kiss to the gentle slope of her neck. She shivered and giggled.

She always had been ticklish there.

It didn't stop him.

He pressed kisses up the curve and one behind her ear, and then dropped one a little lower, closer to the nape of her neck. She shivered for a different reason and tilted her head, angling it away from him and giving him the access he wanted. He took one hand away from her waist and twirled her wavy dark hair up with it, holding it against the back of her head.

Cavanaugh dropped his lips to the nape of her neck and kissed it before licking it, stroking his tongue over the sensitive flesh. A moan slipped from her lips and he couldn't resist the urge that bolted through him.

He opened his mouth, angled his head, and lightly bit the back of her neck with his blunt teeth.

"Cavanaugh!" she barked, her voice echoing across the village.

The singing stopped dead.

She elbowed him in the ribs, but he refused to release her, sinking his teeth in deeper instead, and covered her mouth with one hand, stifling another moan.

He tried not to smile when he heard August's voice loud and clear, telling them to get a room.

Eloise elbowed him again and he released her. She shot to her feet, whirling to face him, her cheeks bright red in the low light.

Cavanaugh did smile now.

He stood and seized hold of her hand, and opened the door behind him. Her scowl fell away as she eyed the open door and then him, and the scent of her desire hit him hard, tearing a growl from him.

He pulled her into the small house, barely giving her time to shut the door before he tugged her towards the thick furs spread out in front of the fireplace in the living room. He released her and she slowed to a halt, her eyes raking over him, making him burn for her.

He waited, staring at her, his chest heaving beneath his jumper and heart labouring as he tried to be patient. He needed to claim her now. He couldn't wait any longer. It had been a struggle to wait for the whole of last night and today, giving her time to make a full recovery, but he didn't have the strength to hold on anymore.

"Eloise," he husked and she answered him by toeing her boots off and stripping out of her jumper.

He smiled as she yanked her top off too and tackled her trousers. Gods, he loved this woman. She was a slave to the same intense passion and need as he was, always primed for him, hungry for another taste.

She frowned when she was standing in only her underwear and he was still fully dressed.

He snapped himself out of it and tugged his jumper off. When his head came free of the neck, Eloise was right in front of him, her fingers making swift work of his trousers. He groaned as she shoved them down and palmed him through his black trunks, making him forget what he had been doing. He stood with his arms still in the air, tangled in his jumper, and his trousers around his knees, lost in how good it felt to have her hand on him, even if it was through a barrier.

Her hand drifted upwards, under his long-sleeve t-shirt and he came back to the world. He was meant to be stripping. He finished with his jumper, grabbed the hem of his t-shirt and pulled it up. Eloise purred.

His knees weakened.

Gods, he wanted her to purr like that when he was inside her.

He tugged his top off and threw it aside, and then stopped dead again as she ran her hands over his chest, slowly exploring it. He moaned and tipped his head back, forgetting everything again when she brought her lips into play, kissing and licking her way down his chest to his stomach.

She swirled her tongue around his navel and he growled when she kneeled on the furs, her face level with his aching shaft.

A wicked glint entered her golden-brown eyes.

Cavanaugh flexed his fingers and reached for his trunks.

Eloise dropped her head and started unlacing his boots. What the hell? Cavanaugh growled again and she giggled. Minx. She wanted to drive him wild, and he was already halfway there, going out of his mind with need.

She carefully removed each of his boots and made him step out of his trousers, and even went as far as taking off his socks for him.

He growled and reached for her, intending to pull her up to him and kiss her until she melted into him. She reached up too, slid her fingers into the waist of his underwear, and he could only stare blankly at her as she pulled it down his thighs, freeing his cock.

It instantly grew harder, as solid as steel and throbbing with need.

He dutifully stepped out of his trunks, his gaze glued to her, waiting to see what she would do next.

She rose onto her knees, wrapped her hand around his length, and then wrapped her mouth around it too. He groaned and swallowed hard as she stroked her tongue over the sensitive head, swirling it around and sending hot shivers shooting down to his balls.

"Eloise," he murmured, closing his eyes and surrendering to her.

She slowly took him into her mouth, her moist heat tearing another low groan from him, and sucked him as she withdrew.

He clasped her head in one hand and guided her on him, breathing hard as he struggled to retain some control. He needed to feel her lips on him, feel his cock sliding into her hot wet mouth, but he had to stay in control and stop himself from surrendering to his urge to thrust, plunging deeper, taking every drop of pleasure she wanted to give to him.

He needed to be inside her when he found release this time, his cock buried in her body and his fangs in the back of her neck.

His balls tightened at just the thought and he pushed her away, breathing hard to calm himself.

She smiled and rose onto her feet, trailing her fingers up his stomach to his chest. He growled and swooped on her mouth when she was close enough, claiming it and slipping his tongue between her lips before she could protest. He kissed her hard and reached around her at the same time. She gasped into his mouth as he snapped the fastenings on her bra and tore it off her. The scent of her arousal grew stronger and he groaned, lowered his hands to her backside and dragged her against him, thrusting his cock against her belly.

"Cavanaugh," she whispered against his lips and he wanted to give in to her, doing as she silently asked him, but he needed to do something else first.

She squealed as he lifted her and turned with her. He kneeled on the furs and laid her down, and broke away from her lips. He trailed his down her throat to her chest and suckled her left nipple, swirling his tongue around it, and then her right as his hands went to work, shoving her underwear down her thighs. She wriggled, bringing her knees up, and he sat back and tugged her knickers down the rest of the way.

Eloise settled her feet on his thighs and smiled as she slowly spread her legs, her hands drifting across her breasts at the same time, her eyes hooded and filled with hunger he wanted to satisfy.

He growled, grabbed her hips, and shoved her up the furs, giving him room. She closed her eyes and threw her head back as he delved between her thighs, sweeping his tongue over her nub, tasting her desire for him.

He moaned and clutched her backside, raising it off the furs, and devoured her, alternating between suckling her sweet bead and flicking it with his tongue.

Eloise arched her back, thrusting her breasts high into the air, and he stared at them, his cock pulsing as he swept his tongue over her, from her core to her nub, tasting all of her. Gods, he needed to be inside her.

He dropped lower, probing her entrance with his tongue, imagining feeding his shaft into her and filling her. His cock throbbed, kicking against his stomach, and he resisted rubbing it against the furs to get some satisfaction. She moaned as he swept back up to her nub and laved it, pressed her feet into the floor, and writhed, rocking against his face. She was close, her body flexing as she sought release.

Cavanaugh couldn't wait any longer.

He flipped her onto her front, pulled her hips up so she was on all fours, and entered her in one smooth stroke, tearing a cry from her lips. He grunted and shifted forwards, plunging deeper still, and pressed his hands into her shoulders, pinning her to the furs. She moaned with the first deep thrust of his cock and bit her lip with the second, igniting a need within him that he had been battling. It burned through him, more powerful than before, laying waste to his restraint.

He slipped his hands beneath her, pulled her up so her back pressed against his chest, and cupped her breasts as he sank his fangs into the back of her neck.

She cried out again, a sharp bark of pleasure that made him growl against her neck. He tightened his grip on her, keeping his fangs in check as best he could, stopping them from becoming too big and damaging her. She moaned and shifted her legs wider, sinking deeper onto him.

He groaned with her and began thrusting, short shallow ones, as much as he could manage while retaining his hold on her. He couldn't let her go. He needed to hold on to his female until she had found release and he had found his too, joining them and awakening the bond between them.

Eloise rocked on him, alternating between rotating her hips and thrusting, her breathing coming quicker. He grunted and pumped harder, shoving deeper into her as he kept hold of her neck, his instincts awakening and beginning to seize control of him. Eloise threw one hand over her head and raked her nails over the back of his neck, ripping a feral growl from him as pleasure blasted down his spine to his balls. He drove harder into her and dropped one hand to her mound, slipping his fingers between her folds to toy with her bundle of nerves as she arched forwards, giving him better access to her body.

He clutched her right breast with his other hand, tweaking her nipple as he plunged into her. Her blood coated his tongue, the sweet taste of her drugging him, making him thrust harder and deeper, a slave to his desire to satisfy his mate. She moaned and moved with him, thrusting against him, her claws scraping the back of his neck as they grew. He shuddered and rocked deeper, grunting each time he slid into her hot sheath, his hips pumping furiously.

His fingers danced between her thighs and she fluttered around him, gasping as she clutched the back of his neck and tipped her head back, pressing it against his.

Cavanaugh bit down harder.

Eloise screamed.

Her body quivered around his as she tensed, gripping him hard both inside her and around the back of his neck. Her release scalded him, hot and slippery as he drove into her, thrusting wildly, pushing her into finding another with him. She jerked forwards and cried out again as he came, spilling himself inside her, his entire body quaking with his release.

Cavanaugh breathed hard against her throat, clutching her to him, his teeth still buried in her neck. She moaned as she sank back into him, her back plastered against his front, and slowly released his neck. She dropped one hand to her lap and one to her breast, catching both of his and slipping her fingers between his, linking them.

He managed to convince himself to let go of her and carefully removed his fangs from the back of her throat. He licked the marks he had left on her, cleaning the blood away.

"I'm sorry," he whispered and wrapped his arms around her, dragging her arms with him. "Did it hurt?"

She shook her head and he licked her wounds again before nuzzling her shoulder. She lifted his hands to her face and kissed them.

Cavanaugh closed his eyes and savoured the sensations building within him, growing stronger with each passing second. Their bond. He could feel it weaving them together.

"Gods, I love you, Eloise," he whispered against her skin and she moved.

He sensed her need and released her, allowing her to pull free of him and come to face him. She settled on his lap, her legs around his waist, and searched his eyes. He could feel all of her emotions, all of her happiness, all of her hope.

All of her love.

He kissed her before she could say the words he had been waiting his entire life to hear, already able to hear them in his heart and his soul through their bond.

She wrapped her arms around his neck and returned the kiss before slowly drawing back and smiling at him, her honey-coloured eyes overflowing with the emotions he could feel in her.

"I love you too, Cavanaugh."

He couldn't stop himself from kissing her again.

Eloise was finally his. It felt like a dream, one he had thought would never come true.

He had a lot to make up for, lost time and a thousand mistakes included.

He was going to spend the rest of his life showing her how much he loved her, and making up for everything he had done wrong and every second they had been apart.

Because he felt like the luckiest son of a bitch alive as he kissed Eloise, aware of the incredible gift she had given him.

She had given him everything he had ever wanted.

She had given him forever.

Forever with her.

The End

ABOUT THE AUTHOR

Felicity Heaton is a New York Times and USA Today best-selling author who writes passionate paranormal romance books. In her books she creates detailed worlds, twisting plots, mind-blowing action, intense emotion and heart-stopping romances with leading men that vary from dark deadly vampires to sexy shape-shifters and wicked werewolves, to sinful angels and hot demons!

If you're a fan of paranormal romance authors Lara Adrian, J R Ward, Sherrilyn Kenyon, Gena Showalter, Larissa Ione and Christine Feehan then you will enjoy her books too.

If you love your angels a little dark and wicked, the best-selling Her Angel series is for you. If you like strong, powerful, and dark vampires then try the Vampires Realm series or any of her stand-alone vampire romance books. If you're looking for vampire romances that are sinful, passionate and erotic then try the best-selling Vampire Erotic Theatre series. Or if you prefer huge detailed worlds filled with hot-blooded alpha males in every species, from elves to demons to dragons to shifters and angels, then take a look at the new Eternal Mates series.

If you have enjoyed this story, please take a moment to contact the author at **author@felicityheaton.co.uk** or to post a review of the book online

Connect with Felicity:
Website – http://www.felicityheaton.co.uk
Blog – http://www.felicityheaton.co.uk/blog/
Twitter – http://twitter.com/felicityheaton
Facebook – http://www.facebook.com/felicityheaton
Goodreads – http://www.goodreads.com/felicityheaton
Mailing List – http://www.felicityheaton.co.uk/newsletter.php

FIND OUT MORE ABOUT HER BOOKS AT:
http://www.felicityheaton.co.uk

Made in the USA
Lexington, KY
31 January 2015